PRETTY ENOUGH

Look for these other books about
The Practically Popular Crowd:

Wanting More
Keeping Secrets
Getting Smart

THE PRACTICALLY POPULAR CROWD

PRETTY ENOUGH

Meg F. Schneider

AN
APPLE
PAPERBACK

SCHOLASTIC INC.
New York Toronto London Auckland Sydney

ISBN 0-590-44804-8

12 11 10 9 8 7 6 5 4 3 2   2 3 4 5 6 7/9

Printed in the U.S.A.   40

First Scholastic printing, October 1992

To my boys,
Adam and Jason

Prologue

Alexa looked around the pizza place nervously. This wasn't going well at all.

She turned her attention back to Barry, who looked ever so slightly bored.

Where had she seen that expression before?

Ah, yes. On Mona. Just yesterday.

What was going on? Was she losing it completely? The most popular girl at Port Andrews Junior High? Sure, she'd never counted herself among the most fascinating people alive. But she had style. She had flash. She could be very entertaining. . . .

At least that's what she'd always thought.

Alexa smiled across the table at Barry.

Maybe it was just a matter of working a bit harder.

What was it Mimi always said? "People need attention."

Okay, then. Alexa's smile broadened.

Trouble was, it was starting to hurt.

1

Margo opened her closet door and frowned. "Fat clothes," she pronounced, looking away with a sigh.

"You have to stop this!" Gina Dumont protested. She began weaving her thin, straight, light-brown hair into a braid. "They're a little roomy. You're not fat. You could lose a few pounds, but so could we all." She paused. "You're obsessed, Margo!"

Margo looked away. Gina didn't get it. No one did.

"You have to stop doing this to yourself! Don't you have some political cause you can worry about?" Gina started to giggle.

"I don't know," Margo sighed with a soft, sad smile. "I liked my old self better, too."

For a moment, Gina fell silent. "Look, you are very cute, and your hair is beautiful. Just look at it." Gina reached up and gently pulled at Margo's thick dark curls. "What I wouldn't give . . . besides, you have the greatest personality. You're

1

vice president of our class. You care about people." She turned and pointed to the collection of local campaign posters that decorated one wall of Margo's cheerful, but messy, red-and-white room. "Everyone loves you."

"Please stop talking about my personality," Margo practically moaned. "Just once, I'd like to be admired for my looks." She pointed at the cover of a teen magazine that was resting on her bed. The perfect image of a slim-figured blonde smiled up at them. "THAT is what I want to look like."

"Who looks like her?" Gina protested with uncharacteristic fierceness. She dangled the magazine from her fingertips as if it were too filthy to touch. "Does anyone? Does she? I mean, without makeup she could look awful!"

"Oh, Margo!" Mrs. Warner's voice rang out from downstairs. "Where's the rest of the girls? Can't wait to see them!"

Instantly, Margo's face fell. She turned to Gina. "Honestly. Sometimes I think she likes you guys more that I do. . . . "

"Don't be silly," Gina replied. "She just wants you to be happy."

Margo was about to argue and then thought better of it. Gina would never understand. She had the opposite problem. Her strict European parents thought she socialized too much. How could she possibly understand having a mother who thought being "Miss Georgia Peach" in college had been the high point of her life?

Margo smiled at her friend. "What my mother really wants is Alexa for a daughter." And with that she placed both hands on her hips and sashayed across the room. "Oh, hello!" She waved at an imaginary friend. "Lunch today?!" she called out to another. "Now, boys . . . wait your turn," she admonished a supposed crowd.

"What's going on!" a familiar voice called out.

Margo turned around to find Priscilla Levitt standing in the doorway. She threw back her head and laughed. "Need you ask? I was just doing my Alexa act." Margo flopped down on the red-and-white pin-striped comforter that covered her double bed.

Priscilla nodded. "It wasn't bad. But you forgot the most important part." Quickly, she threw her books and art portfolio on the bed, shook her long, chestnut hair until a piece partially covered one eye and, wearing a very bored expression on her face, slowly drawled, "Yes . . . what is it?" in her best "What-do-you-want-now" voice.

Margo grinned. "You do that SO well. . . ." She could just see Alexa Craft now. The most admired girl in school. Blonde, blue-eyed, thin, and gorgeous. It wasn't fair. She'd treated them all so badly. Alexa had befriended every single girl in The Practically Popular Crowd last year, and one by one she'd dropped them all. No reason. No excuses. A clean break each time.

Except for one thing. Alexa knew a bit too much about each one of them. It was a dangerous state of affairs.

"So, do you like?" Priscilla asked, pivoting.

Margo nodded enthusiastically as she admired the lavender flowers Priscilla had hand painted on her navy blue jacket. They were almost as striking as Priscilla. Her graceful height, thick brown hair naturally streaked with blonde, strong features, and large green eyes were hard to miss.

"It's great looking," Margo smiled, and then began fishing through her desk drawer for the notebook marked THE PRACTICALLY POPULAR CROWD. The drawer was stuffed with so many notes, cards, political brochures, pictures, and campaign buttons, she finally had to pull it out and dump the entire contents on the floor.

"Good gracious." Priscilla practically recoiled. "Do you keep animals in there?"

Margo heaved a sigh and stared at the mess. This was definitely not one of her better days. Once again, she turned to study Priscilla. She had such style. Such funk. Margo looked down at her own oversized bright-red sweater. She felt like a balloon. "I want to be glamorous!" she suddenly blurted out. "And I want long legs." She grinned broadly, as if it were a joke, which it absolutely wasn't.

4

It was a drag. Obsessing about looks wasn't fun. She wished it would go away. But how could it, with all those reminders? Why was it all the girls on TV looked so glamorous?

"I think you have a nice body," Gina insisted. "You're not built like a model, but so what?"

"Easy for you to say," Margo responded as she began sifting through the mess on the floor. "You're tall. You're athletic. You're almost blonde. Half of the high school basketball team has a crush on you." She paused. "Your mother didn't win any beauty pageants."

"Here it is!" Priscilla called out triumphantly, pulling the notebook out from under a pile of papers on Margo's night table.

"And here we are," called out Michelle Horne and Vivienne Bennis almost in unison, as the last two members of The Practically Popular Crowd trooped into Margo's room.

"Close the door," Margo whispered. She was certain her mother hung outside, anxious to hear all their secrets.

Vivienne nodded silently, softly clicked the door shut, and then self-consciously wrapped her long jean coat around her still-boyish figure. She grinned. "Why is it every time we have a meeting here, I feel like I'm in the middle of a spy movie?"

"Because my mother wants to know everything about my life," Margo answered matter-of-factly.

"That's not totally true," Priscilla replied softly.

5

"So she can brag about it to her friends. . . . " Margo continued. "My daughter's as popular as I was!" she said in her best Mrs. Warner imitation. Margo shook her head. "Honestly, I wish she'd get a boyfriend and leave me alone. I mean, she's not the first widow in the world. . . . "

"Margo!" Gina protested. "That sounds so cold-hearted!"

Margo looked away. She hadn't meant it that way. But her father had been dead nine years, and it was hard being the center of a beauty queen's attention. Lewis was lucky. The son of a beauty queen could get away with murder.

"Well, Margo's probably partly right, Gina," Michelle interjected. "She does spend a lot of time pushing Margo."

Margo shot Michelle a thankful look. Michelle was really good at understanding people.

"Anyway," Michelle went on, "I've got big news. Let's start the meeting. Okay?"

All the girls settled into a circle on the floor, and Margo reached for her notebook. For a moment, she studied the lettering on the cover — THE PRATICALLY POPULAR CROWD, EIGHTH GRADE — and smiled. The Crowd had been formed for so many reasons. To help each other feel good about themselves. To support each other in bad times. To stand up for each other and help each other be the very best they could possibly be. And it was working, even though they were so different from each other. Priscilla was always direct, a talented artist, and often seemed the most serious and mature of them all. Michelle played great flute and was very smart about people. Vivienne was the brains of the outfit, who hid a lot of insecurity behind long words and tough talk. Boys hadn't yet entered her life at all. And then there was Gina. Quiet. Athletic. Never one to let her real feelings show. Yet, somehow they had all clicked. They all truly cared about each other.

"So, can I start?" Michelle was practically gyrating on the floor.

"Yes," Margo nodded, scrawling *Monday, October 15th* across the top of an empty page. "Go ahead."

"Well, a sign was posted outside the principal's office announcing that Gerrards, the big department store, is planning a special teen fashion show and wants to use kids from local schools to model! Can you believe it? Auditions are in a little over a week! I'm dying to try out!" Instantly, Michelle jumped up, threw open the closet door, and studied herself in the mirror. "I don't know. Maybe I'm being ridiculous." She shook her head a bit and watched her shoulder-length dark brown hair fall into place.

"No, you are not," Priscilla said firmly. "If you think you'd enjoy it, do it! You're a perfect size seven. You're very cute. Why not?"

7

"Why don't we all try out?" Michelle replied excitedly.

"Personally, I think modeling is for the intellectually limited," Vivienne shrugged. "Which you are definitely not. But, hey, who am I? What do you think, Margo?"

Margo looked around the room. Actually, she was thinking a lot of things. And uppermost on the list was how much she would give to dazzle a roomful of people with her grace and beauty.

And how happy it would make her mother.

And how useless it was to think it could happen.

"I believe," Margo finally answered with forced brightness, "that Michelle should go for it. I do. I see no reason why she wouldn't be chosen."

"Well, let's not go that far," Vivienne interjected. "I mean, how many girls are they looking for? How many are trying out? You can't ignore statistics."

"True," Priscilla grinned. "But you can't ignore Michelle's determination, either!"

"Or our help!" Gina laughed. "I'd love to put a little makeup on you, Michelle."

"And I could help you put together a great outfit. Something unusual and eye-catching," Priscilla added.

"Count me out." Vivienne held up both hands. "The most I can do is some quick computation to let you know if you have half a chance."

Finally, all eyes settled on Margo.

She smiled at her friends. "I'll do whatever you want," she said, dramatically spreading her arms out wide. "You know that. Michelle, you'll be the best-looking one up there."

Then she looked down at her notebook and wrote, "We agree to help Michelle win a spot in Gerrard's fashion show. Gina will do make-up, Priscilla clothes, Vivienne statistics, and Margo . . . "

Margo pursed her lips and thought hard. Finally, she scrawled the word "whatever." She looked up, suddenly desperate to change the subject. It hurt too much.

"So . . . what else do we have to talk about today?" she asked, forcing a big smile.

"Well, wait. What's the rush?" Michelle asked incredulously. "I'm not through."

"Sorry," Margo murmured. "I didn't realize . . . "

She looked down at the notebook once more and frowned.

But of course she had realized. Many things.

Like, for instance, it was nice having a great personality.

But long legs and a tiny waist . . . now, that would have been heaven.

2

"Is this not great?!" Alexa exclaimed, jabbing her finger excitedly at the fashion show announcement. "Can you think of anything more fun?" She sucked in her stomach. What a Tuesday this was turning out to be.

"It's good," Mona nodded with only mild interest. Once again she began flipping through her notebook marked DEBATE.

Alexa gave her best friend a sideward glance and frowned. There it was again. She said red. Mona said pink. She said big. Mona said medium. They just weren't seeing things quite the same way anymore.

Or maybe they never had.

Alexa shuddered at the thought. Mona was her most trusted friend in the world. Sure, it looked as if she had tons of buddies, but she didn't really. It's just that she was always surrounded. It made for a busy schedule. But that was all. Alexa hardly opened up to anyone. In fact, she often hid her thoughts from Mona. Alexa tried again.

10

"Do you want to do it with me? Mona, it would be so much fun! Think of the clothes. Think of the attention! Think of what the boys would think!" She reached out and gave Mona's rich dark hair a playful tug. "You're ultra good-looking, you know. Very . . . mysterious."

Mona shook her head. "I can't. I really can't, Alexa. You do it. I've got too much going on with the debate team. I've got to read up on the Gulf War." She reached for Alexa's hand. "If you need me for anything, just let me know."

Alexa nodded. "Yeah. Sure," she answered, gently pulling her hand away. Something was definitely wrong. What was Mona's problem, anyway? And here she had complimented her so nicely, too. Mona used to love doing everything with Alexa. They used to have so much fun. But now . . .

"Well." Alexa checked her watch. "I've got gym. I'll see you later." She shot Mona a quick smile and then looked down the hall. Her friend Robin was standing by her locker near the stairway.

"Robin!" Alexa rushed forward. Now here was someone she could always count on. She was fun, too. And she ALWAYS loved to be with Alexa. Next to Mona, Robin was her closest friend.

"Alexa, I know what you're going to say!" Robin called out. "I saw it, and you're perfect!"

Alexa hesitated. Yes. Robin was a pal. Except for one thing.

11

Robin agreed with everything. It wasn't real. She always did what Alexa wanted. She always said what Alexa wanted to hear. It just didn't feel right.

Alexa sighed. She couldn't win. One friend was suddenly living her own life, and it drove her crazy. One friend "yessed" Alexa to death, and that didn't feel much better.

What was a friend, anyway?

"They should see you now!" Robin continued warmly and loudly. "You look great today!"

"Thanks," Alexa smiled, tossing her long, thick blonde hair behind her shoulders as she arrived at Robin's side.

Well, so far Robin was being honest. She did look great. The snug ice-blue long-sleeved tee she had tucked into a pair of white corduroy pants seemed to set her complexion aglow.

"I have to say I'm pretty excited," Alexa smiled.

"I don't blame you," Robin grinned. "It had your name written all over it."

"I wouldn't go that far," Alexa replied dryly. Enough was enough. She cocked her head to one side and studied her friend. "You know, you could try out, too. . . . "

"You think so?!" Robin exclaimed with a huge smile. Then she shook her head. "Nah. I'm not the type."

For a moment, Alexa considered arguing with

12

her and then changed her mind. The truth was, Robin probably wasn't the type. She was definitely cute. Her short curly hair, bright blue eyes, and curvy figure created an appealing picture. Guys had certainly started noticing her. But she was also a little on the klutzy side. And short.

Instead, Alexa shrugged her shoulders. "Up to you," she said mildly. Once again, she checked her watch. "The bell's about to ring. I've got gym." And with that, she started to walk away.

"Hi, Alexa!" James Wood called out from down the hall. She waved in his direction.

"Lunch, Alexa?" Julie asked, grabbing her arm for an instant. Alexa nodded.

Keeping her shoulders back and her head high, as if she were already modeling the latest fashion, Alexa continued down the hall.

If only Barry Drake could see her now. So popular. So admired. So pretty.

Alexa frowned. But he had seen all that.

And he still looked bored.

She shrugged. Come to think of it, he didn't really excite her, either.

Nor did his friends. David, with his wicked sense of humor, which was usually aimed at Alexa, drove her crazy. He wasn't nearly as cute as Barry. Where did he come off?

Well, often these things took time. After all, Barry and she were the perfect couple. Or so it seemed. She actually didn't know him that well.

They'd met at a swim meet. Not that she hadn't noticed him before. His name was everywhere. He was a star. As was she. He had looks and brains, and she had looks and, well, smarts. People smarts.

They were bound to hit it off, and this modeling thing was the perfect opportunity to really get things going. One look at her on the runway and he'd melt. Then all she'd have to do was be reasonably interesting and fun. That was easy enough.

Alexa held her head high as she climbed the stairs.

Still, too bad looks weren't everything. She'd be the happiest person on earth.

3

"Honey, I'll be off in a second," Aurora Warner whispered, covering the phone mouthpiece with her hand. "Sit down somewhere."

Margo turned and looked around the busy River Realty office where Mrs. Warner worked. A few feet away she spotted an empty office chair and, settling herself into it, Margo proceeded to study her mother.

She sighed. Mrs. Warner was still very attractive, though rather heavy now. Still, Margo could easily imagine her, twenty years ago, perched on top of a convertible holding a dozen roses and waving at the crowds. How Mr. Warner must have loved her. Margo tried to envision the look on his face as he gazed at his future wife. Thick blonde hair shining in the sun, long slender legs exposed for all to see. Margo looked down at her own legs. They weren't bad. But they certainly weren't anything to write home about.

For a moment, she tried to imagine herself sitting atop a fancy car, glistening crown arranged in her unruly curls, waving to the adoring crowds. Somehow it didn't compute.

"Absolutely," Mrs. Warner's cheery voice interrupted her thoughts. "It's a delicious house! The rooms are so open and filled with light, and of course there's plenty of room to build on. I'm happy to take you back for another look whenever you want tomorrow. . . . "

Margo smiled. Her mother could be so charming. So persistent. So — Margo frowned — pushy. In business, it was great. With daughters, it was a nightmare. Why couldn't her mother turn all that energy into thinking about her own personal life instead of Margo's? And why couldn't she bother Margo's brother, Lewis, a little? So he was a boy. So he was a senior in high school. So what?

Margo shook her head. That was easy. Because Lewis wasn't expected to carry on the Kelly "belle of the ball" tradition.

"Margo? Margo, honey?"

Margo looked up to find her mother waving her over.

"I'm done! Time for dinner. What's it going to be tonight? Italian, seafood, or burgers?"

Margo considered the options. It had become a tradition for the two of them to go out for dinner on Tuesday nights. Sometimes Lewis came, but most times not. At first, it had been fun. But, lately, Margo had begun to wonder what would happen if one night she had to do something else. She had the uncomfortable feeling her mother's world would fall apart.

"Well? Come on," Mrs. Warner urged her. "I'm starved. Make up your mind."

"Burgers," Margo replied. "Joanna's. The place with the salad bar." She looked down at her long baggy black jacket. Fat clothes. For a moment, she considered saying, "I'd like to lose some weight," but stopped herself. Her mother would be on a roll. By the morning she'd have Margo enrolled in an exercise class, diet course, and booked for an appointment at the beauty parlor for a "whole new look."

Smiling pleasantly at her mother, Margo turned to walk toward the office front door. Better to keep her secret thoughts to herself. The Practically Popular Crowd was one thing. Miss Georgia Peach was quite another.

Alexa looked across the table at her parents and burst into a huge smile. The three of them hadn't had dinner together for so long. She glanced at the menu. Joanna's. Her favorite place. Wait until she told them her news. They'd be so impressed.

"Anyway," Alexa began, placing both hands on the table. "I have something to . . . "

"Hmmm," Sam Craft interrupted. "Just a sec, Lexa. This menu sure looks good. I'm almost glad the stove isn't working."

"Just as long as it's back in shape for my dinner party," Alissa Craft sighed.

"You're giving a party?" Alexa asked. "Anyone famous coming?"

"No, dear," Mrs. Craft smiled. "Just a small thing in honor of a cameraman I do a lot of work with. Say, isn't that Margo Warner and her mother?" She looked at her husband. "She's a realtor, you know. She could probably help out that customer of yours you were telling me about."

Alexa turned around. It sure was the Warner family. Alexa looked back at her menu, feeling the not-so-old anger begin to stir. It had been a few weeks since the Michelle Horne/Michael Phillips fiasco. But she certainly hadn't forgotten. How could they have tricked her so completely? It was positively . . . diabolical. Alexa frowned.

And absolutely no opportunity had yet presented itself for her to put any of her own plans for revenge into motion.

None. Alexa turned once more and studied Mrs. Warner. Except, just maybe, now.

"Are you ready?" A pleasant young waitress arrived at the Craft table and looked around expectantly.

"I'll take the T-bone with a baked potato," Mr. Craft declared. "Make it rare, please."

"I'll just have a mushroom burger," Mrs. Craft said slowly. "No potatoes, please."

Alexa considered the menu before her. One hamburger was something like 130 calories. And that didn't include the bun, which was about seventy-five, not to mention the slice of cheese, which was about a hundred calories, most of which was fat. Alexa glanced over at the salad bar. At the moment, Margo and her mother were busily filling their plates. Mrs. Warner. Now there was a difficult mother. Sure, Mrs. Craft wasn't home a lot. But at least when she was, she didn't spend her time trying to make Alexa into someone she wasn't.

Again, a vision of Michael Phillips danced before her.

It was Michelle who she really wanted to ruin. Michelle or Vivienne. For a moment, she studied Margo. Still, they had all been in on it. That Almost Popular Bunch, or whatever they called themselves. Nope, she was tired of waiting. She'd just cause Margo a little trouble tonight to start the ball rolling. She'd get to everyone else later. No hurry, really. She had all year. At least.

"Ummm, I'll stick to salad," Alexa murmured. "Excuse me. I'm starving."

Alexa stood up and headed for the salad bar.

Margo was filling a dinner-sized plate. That could mean only one thing. She was on a diet. Alexa grinned. Gerrard's fashion show. Margo really wasn't the type. Still, there could be a connection.

At any rate, it was a good place to start.

"Mrs. Warner!" Alexa sang out. "How nice to see you again. Hello, Margo."

"Hi," Margo answered, flashing Alexa a suspicious look.

"Salads for everyone, I see," Alexa went on brightly. "Just too many calories in meat, I guess. . . ."

"Alexa, you don't need to worry about your weight," Mrs. Warner chimed in. "You look just lovely. Why haven't I seen you around our house lately?"

Alexa shot Margo a quick glance. So, nothing had changed. Here were a mother and daughter who never talked. If there was anyone who could recognize those signs, it was Alexa. For an instant she almost went back to her seat. Still. Alexa hesitated. Sympathy had no place here. Margo had done her wrong. And to think they used to be friends.

"Oh, I don't know, Mrs. Warner." She took a deep breath and turned to Margo. "So, what about that teen fashion show at Gerrards! Are you going to try out?" She glanced quickly at Mrs. Warner to make sure she was listening.

"Oh, I don't think . . . " Margo let her voice trail off uncomfortably as she reached for a spoonful of radishes.

"You're not?" Alexa insisted. "So, why the salad bar? Let's face it. Joanna's hamburgers are the best!"

"What fashion show is this, Margo?" Mrs. Warner asked, one hand suspended, completely still, over the carrot bowl. "It sounds delicious!"

"It's nothing, Mom. Really. I'm not interested." Margo shot Alexa an angry glance.

Alexa smiled. She could actually stop now. Margo's mother would probably be at her all night. Still, one more thing . . .

"Everyone's trying out, Mrs. Warner," Alexa added for good measure. "There are lots of openings." Then she shrugged and reached for a plate. "Well. Time to eat. Enjoy yourselves."

And with that, Alexa walked to the opposite side of the huge salad bar and started enthusiastically loading up. She could hear Margo's and Mrs. Warner's urgent whispers as she made her way around the table. Alexa smiled and studied her plate. Carrots, radishes, asparagus, chopped egg, scallions, pasta shells. A little of this, a little of that. Salad bars were so much fun. She looked up at Margo. For so many reasons.

"Well, dear, that looks colorful and interesting,"

Mrs Craft commented as Alexa arrived back at the table.

"Doesn't it, though." Alexa nodded, her eyes glued to Margo and her mother as they engaged in what was clearly a very tense conversation.

"So . . . " Alexa began, turning her attention back to her parents. "Want to hear about what happened today at school?"

"We do, dear." Mr. Craft nodded. "Tell us?"

"Well, Gerrards is having a teen fashion show and is looking to use girls from the local schools to model. I'm trying out next week. Isn't that exciting?"

"Darling! That's wonderful." Mrs. Craft smiled warmly at her daughter. "And you know, if you're chosen, we'll do our very best to be there."

Alexa smiled and nodded. Very best. What did that mean?

"You bet," Mr. Craft nodded. "I wouldn't want to miss that."

Alexa's smile broadened. That was better.

"Anyway, Alissa," Mr. Craft went on speaking to his wife. "Finish the story you were telling me."

"Oh, but wait. Don't you want to know the . . . " Alexa practically sputtered.

"In a minute, honey. Your mother was telling me something important when you came back to the table."

"Sure," Alexa nodded. She waited as her mother continued describing a crisis at work.

She began lightly nibbling on her salad, waiting for a pause in the conversation. Five minutes later, she began to wolf the salad down. There wasn't much else to do.

Her mother's story was turning out to be VERY long.

4

Margo closed the door to her room and heaved a sigh of relief. It could have been worse. Her mother had only spent about ten minutes trying to talk her into the fashion show. That wasn't bad at all. Not when you considered they sat across the table from each other for an entire meal, not twenty feet away from the beautiful Alexa and her still-gorgeous mother. Margo tossed her bag on the desk chair.

Now *there* was a mom who left her daughter alone. What a pleasure that must be. Probably they chatted about "girl" things a lot.

Margo felt a familiar tug of sadness. Actually, she wanted to talk about "girl" things, too. But she couldn't. Not with her mother. She'd tried it once. Not too long ago. She'd asked her mother what style skirt she thought was best for her. Suddenly, they were talking about how pretty Margo could be if only she did this or that, and then Margo had had to sit through yet another telling of the Kelly girl tradition.

Aurora Kelly Warner. Daughter of Elizabeth Jamison Kelly.

Both pageant winners.

Both eager to pass on the glory.

And then the unspoken part. Both waiting for Margo Eleanore Kelly Warner to get her act together.

It had been a horrible feeling. She was a disappointment. She was a failure. It made her very sad.

It made her very angry.

"How's my gorgeous grandaughter?" Grandma Kelly would ask each time Margo answered the phone.

"You don't have one," Margo always wanted to answer.

Why couldn't they leave her alone?

Margo lay down on her bed and closed her eyes. In fact, why couldn't she leave herself alone? Lately, she'd begun standing in front of mirrors, any mirror, and looking. Watching. Waiting to feel beautiful. As if nothing else counted. As if Margo Warner had nothing else in the world to offer. Daydreams had begun haunting her every move.

There she was, dazzling in an off-the-shoulder prom dress she'd never have the nerve to wear. Her long slender legs, which didn't resemble hers at all, were now taking the runway. Her thick lustrous dark curls, gathered on top of her head, in a way they never would, sparkled in the spot-lights. And her tiny waist shown off by a single silk rose sewn . . .

Margo's eyes flew open at the sound of a gentle knock on her door.

"Honey, can I come in?"

Margo closed her eyes once more. Pretending to be asleep usually worked well.

"Sweetie, you can't be asleep yet!" the voice persisted louder now.

Margo sighed. It was true. She was still dressed. "Come in," Margo called out sullenly. "I didn't hear you. I had my headphones on," she added, quickly pulling them off her desk and onto her bed.

Mrs. Warner walked in and sat down on the edge of Margo's bed. "I want to talk with you about something."

Margo nodded. Funny. She had really thought she'd heard the end of it. How foolish of her.

"I don't believe you about the fashion show. Are you sure you wouldn't just love to be in it?"

Well, you're partly right and partly wrong, Margo thought to herself. Mostly, though, YOU want to be in it.

"Well, you're wrong," Margo insisted out loud. She looked away, desperate to get back to that glorious image she'd conjured up only moments ago. What was the matter with her mother, any-way? What was the point? Why couldn't she see she just didn't have a Miss Georgia Peach for a daughter?

"I don't think I am, and I'd like to help you if you'd let me. You are lovely looking, you know."

"I'm not the modeling type," Margo blurted out more loudly than she had intended. "Is that so terrible?"

"Nonsense. All Kelly girls are the modeling type," Mrs. Warner smiled dreamily, ignoring the question. Wonderful or terrible was apparently not the issue.

"Mom," Margo finally snapped. "Why don't YOU try out?"

"Honey," Mrs Warner continued, without missing a beat, "I know you need to lose a few pounds. And I know you're not a classic beauty like . . . like . . . "

"Alexa," Margo suggested sarcastically.

"Well, no. I was thinking of Christie Brinkley."

Margo laughed in spite of the small sting. "No, I'm not that." It was funny. It was one thing to know she wasn't a classic beauty. It was another to hear her own mother confirm the fact.

Margo looked back at Mrs. Warner, who was now studying her hands with a sad expression on her face. Margo turned away. Why was it that her mother always made her feel like a traitor?

"I just think you should do it this once," Mrs Warner whispered. "You might be surprised."

"You mean shocked."

"You have a very warped opinion of yourself."

"But, Mom," Margo finally sighed. She was just too exhausted to keep it up entirely. "Even if I wanted to try, they'd never pick me. . . . " She looked away. Well, there it was. The bottom line. She did want to try. But she knew, absolutely, she'd never walk down the runway.

"Ah ha!" Suddenly, Mrs. Warner was on her feet. "Don't you see? Looks is just a small part of it. It's the attitude that counts more! If you feel good, you'll look good." She stepped over to a mirror. "I was never a classic beauty, either. But I had style. And that's what you're going to have."

"But look at me . . . " Margo began to protest.

"I am looking at you," Mrs Warner turned and studied her daughter. "Tomorrow the diet begins. You have one week to lose a few pounds. I'll make an appointment with my hairdresser for you. The day before the audition, we'll go shopping for something new." She crossed both hands across her chest. "Sweetie, it does no good to pretend you don't want something when you do. I'm thrilled." And with that, she walked out the door.

"I know you are," Margo whispered. Then she stood up and looked in the mirror. She closed her eyes and brought back the beautiful image of her taking the runway with long legs, slim waist, and magnificently coiffed hair.

It WAS a thrill.

Maybe she could try.

The truth was, if she could make the dream come true, nothing would make her happier. Or her mother.

It was a a beautiful thought.

She frowned. For a not-so-beautiful girl.

Alexa sat cross-legged on her bed, waiting for the phone at her feet to ring. Barry had said he'd call. So far, he'd been very reliable. She began drumming her fingertips on the receiver. Not that she was looking forward to the call or anything. The conversations never flowed very well on the phone.

Well, actually, they didn't in person, either. . . .

Alexa checked her watch. Eight o'clock. She picked up a pen and paper and began making notes.

THINGS TO TALK ABOUT

Alexa began sucking on the end of the pen. Finally, she put pen to paper.

The basketball game against Bridgetown.

The high school science club exhibit.

Alexa hesitated, and then crossed out the exhibit. She didn't like science and wouldn't be able to discuss a thing.

The fashion show.

Mrs. Simon's math test.

She put the pen down. That was enough. Alexa was about to stand up when the phone rang.

"Hello," she said softly, anxious to sound hopelessly feminine. She ran a hand over the white-and-lavender bedspread.

"Hi, Alexa," Barry's familiar warm voice replied.

Alexa smiled. "So, how was your day?" She grimaced. The question sounded SO ordinary.

"Good," he replied emphatically. "I chose my science project."

"Great," Alexa replied, feeling her whole body tense. "What is it?"

"Oh, I think I want to build a cross section of a space shuttle. I love using my hands, and I'm fascinated by the engineering of the thing."

"Sounds wonderful," Alexa offered. That was, after all, a safe comment.

"Well, I don't know if I'd call it wonderful," Barry commented. "But it should be challenging. Do you have any idea how many small parts I have to build or draw in to show where all the critical mechanisms are?"

Alexa was afraid to speak. "Wonderful" had been the wrong word. Was "No" the right word here? Or what about, "Tell me"?

The trouble with "Tell me" was, she really wasn't interested.

Alexa frowned.

"I don't know much about space shuttles," Alexa finally commented after a long pause. "But I'd like to learn," she added. That wasn't even slightly true, but it seemed right.

He laughed. "I'll lend you a book I have on the subject. Somehow, Alexa, I don't think it's your thing."

Alexa giggled, not exactly sure if she was being insulted or not. It wasn't a pleasant sensation. She checked her list.

The fashion show.

She was just about to give him the news when it struck her that going from space shuttles to clothes didn't seem right. Mrs. Simon's math test was a better fit.

"I have Mrs. Simon this year," Alexa began. "Did you have her in eighth grade? She's tough."

"Fair, though," Barry replied. "Her tests are hard."

"Exactly!" Alexa exclaimed. Terrific. They were about to thoroughly agree. "I took one today, and I swear she was quizzing us on stuff we hadn't gotten to yet!"

"Impossible," Barry replied. "She's too careful for that. But she does make up tricky problems."

"Well, of course that's what I meant," Alexa replied defensively. She sighed and checked her watch. This was exhausting. It was easier when they were together. When the conversation didn't go smoothly, there were still other things to do. Like go to the movies. Or watch a sports event. Or kiss.

Something was wrong.

Still, there had to be a way. Barry was just too good a catch. Didn't Mimi say relationships took work? Yes. She always said that.

Alexa frowned.

But she couldn't have meant this much. . . .

"By the way," Barry went on. "Someone here wants to talk with you."

"Had a hard time with the math test?"

Alexa cringed. David. "Yes," Alexa replied carefully.

"Well, don't worry. Everyone does."

"Really?" Alexa blurted out. "I'm not so good at math."

"Yes, well, I meant everyone who isn't good at math has a problem."

"You're impossible," Alexa snapped. "I'm hanging up." Why did he have to embarrass her this way? Weren't things bad enough?

"I'm just teasing," David said gently. "I had trouble with her tests all the time and I'm good at math."

Alexa was afraid to speak. It felt like a trap.

"You've got to lighten up," David went on. "A person would think you think you're dumb."

"I'm not dumb," Alexa murmured. Darn him. In front of Barry, too.

"Oh, I know that, Alexa," David said with a smile in his voice. "You're very sharp. I just don't think you know it." He paused. "Here's Barry. I'm getting off."

Alexa nodded.

But for a split second she wished he wouldn't.

5

"That's terrific!" Michelle squealed. "We can do it together!" She practically jumped up and down in the girls' bathroom.

"Well, you mean we can try out together," Margo cautioned. "I mean, let's face it. I'm not . . . " She hesitated. "Christie Brinkley." Self-consciously, she looked down at her baggy jeans and stylish, but loose, turtleneck sweater.

"Yeah, well, neither am I," Michelle giggled. "But who cares?"

"I can help you work out a healthy diet," Gina volunteered. "Low fat. High carbohydrates. That kind of thing." Her blue eyes sparkled with determination.

Margo nodded. "Let's see. Today is Wednesday. We have a week. You think I can lose five pounds? I mean, I need to lose ten, but five would help." She checked herself in the mirror. "I'm not bad looking, really, am I?"

She ran a hand through her hair. She wasn't.

It's just that this felt so . . . so . . . unlike her.

"Look," Priscilla said, yanking open her portfolio. "Stand still."

Quickly, she pulled out her sketch pad, turned Margo's face so she was looking at her profile, and began to sketch. Everyone was silent. A minute later she held up her work.

"You see! Look at that profile. Your nose is beautiful, you have nice cheekbones that will stick out even more when you lose weight, and you have pretty round green eyes."

Margo studied the sketch. She didn't look bad. Still, the truth was she didn't have a model's body, and her face, though very nice, wasn't exactly exotic. It was open. Friendly. Like the girl next door.

"The question is," Margo sighed, "what happens if I'm not chosen? What do I do then?"

"What do you mean, what will you do?" Priscilla asked with surprise. "You'll keep being wonderful Margo. And you'll be five pounds thinner to boot!"

"Easy for you to say," Margo shivered. "And what do I do about my mother . . . " Suddenly, she broke into a huge smile. "I know! I'll get a wig that looks like my hair, you can wear it, I'll misplace my mother's glasses, and we'll tell her you're me!"

"There. You see? There's always a solution," Priscilla joked back.

Margo smiled softly and then looked away. How could she explain that if she didn't win a spot in the show, she'd be losing for two people?

Make that three. Grandma Kelly was all the way down in Georgia, but somehow she always seemed nearby.

Margo stood in front of the classroom and waited for everyone to settle down. She checked her watch. It was almost time to start the meeting. She cleared her throat. Funny thing. It wasn't her role to preside over a mandatory class meeting. It was the president's job. But Lisa Meade was sick, and so here she was. And she wasn't even nervous. Sixty kids were looking at her expectantly, and she didn't mind at all.

"Okay, then," she began, "I'd like to call this meeting into session." She paused, waiting for the last whispering to stop. Then she joked, "And I'd like to call Margo Warner forward, as she is responsible for masterminding all of our community projects." Margo paused and waited for the laughter that lightly filled the room to die out. Then she cleared her throat. "We have to choose a charity for the fall bake sale." She picked up a pointer resting underneath the blackboard and pointed to a list of organizations she'd drawn up. "These are the organizations we've discussed before."

"What about the Port Andrews basketball

team?" Paul Harmon's voice called out. "We need new jerseys!"

The class began to laugh, Margo included.

"I need a new wardrobe myself," she joked. She looked around the room. "Any other brilliant ideas?" she asked with a big smile.

"I think we should use the money to hire a new cook," a voice called out from the back. "Did anyone taste that chicken chow mein yesterday?" Again everyone cracked up.

Margo grinned. "Not me."

"I wonder why. . . . " Alexa's voice shot through the air.

For an extremely brief moment, Margo froze. Then her eyes settled on Michelle, who was almost imperceptibly shaking her head as if to say, "Forget it. Don't get upset. Let it go."

Margo hesitated, and then smiled serenely.

"Because, Alexa," she began, "I skipped lunch. I was too busy in the school office researching the organizations you see before you." She paused again. "In short, I had better things to do."

"Ooooooooooooooooooooo," a few voices called out in unison, and once again the class was rocked with laughter. Margo stole a look at Michelle, who flashed her a huge grin.

"Now," Margo said, standing before the board, "let's discuss which organization, at this point, appears to be the neediest, and for what. And then let's take a vote."

It was weird how she could take command of most things, but when it came to her looks, or her mother, she simply fell apart.

Alexa stood at the baseline and eyed her opponent. It was Robin, actually, but on the tennis court, Alexa had no friends. She just liked to win.

Tossing the ball in the air, she aimed for an ace, but it didn't come together. She slowed down and took it a little easier this time. No point double faulting.

Robin returned the serve easily, and Alexa made a long, low ground stroke back to the baseline. Again, Robin was there.

Alexa didn't like that. Robin wasn't nearly as athletic or graceful or fast as she was. This time she pulled in her shot, making it land just on the other side of the net. Robin, expecting another long low shot, ran forward, but not quickly enough.

"15–0" Alexa called out, and then quickly turned, in an effort to hide her triumphant smile.

"Thought I'd find you here," a familiar voice called out. Alexa looked up to find Mona standing off to the side of the court. Alexa looked down at her racket nonchalantly and pretended to straighten the strings.

"Hi," she said matter-of-factly.

"Sorry I've been so busy," Mona went on, "but

you know the debate is in only three weeks, and I've been studying and practicing a lot."

"I know." Alexa smiled ever so slightly at her friend. "You've got to do what you've got to do."

"How's the fashion thing going?" Mona asked. "Any news?"

"News?" Alexa chuckled sarcastically. "I told you. The auditions are next week. No new news." She hesitated. "Barry and I are doing pretty well, though."

Mona nodded. "Oh. I'm glad that's going better."

Alexa eyed her carefully. That didn't sound very nice. What did she mean, "better"? Like she noticed things were "worse"? And who was she, anyway, to know how two people were getting along when she was hardly around? So what if she couldn't quite call Barry her boyfriend? Yet. Alexa opened her mouth to say so, when something stopped her. She didn't like arguing with Mona. Not that their friendship ever really seemed to fall apart when they did. It just made her lonely. Alexa cocked her head to one side. I'm being too hard. Too distant. Maybe that's it.

"Would you like to help me with my makeup and stuff right before the tryouts?" Alexa asked, softening somewhat.

"Well . . . sure." Mona replied hesitantly. "When?"

"Next Wednesday at four o'clock."

"Oh." Mona's face grew serious. "I can't. I have a practice session then . . . "

"Fine." Alexa shrugged. "I understand. Look, I can't help you, either. . . . "

"Actually, you probably could . . . " Mona replied hopefully.

Alexa felt herself growing angry. "Right. You need me to help you with a debate on a subject I know little about and at this point care about even less. Right." What did Mona take her for, a fool? If there was one thing Alexa was very clear about, it was her strengths and weaknesses.

And with that, she turned around and called out to Robin. "Ready?"

Robin was now halfway across the court on her way toward joining her friends. For a moment she hesitated, and then turned around to take up position. Once again, Alexa tried to ace the serve.

It was in. Still, she felt terrible.

Mona, it seemed, was on her way out.

6

"**O**kay, now, heads straight, shoulders back, start forward." Priscilla clapped her hands together for effect. "Keep your eyes focused on one thing for balance." Her brightly colored peasant skirt swayed gracefully as she motioned them forward.

Margo nodded as she again made her way across the Warners' overdecorated living room Saturday morning. Her eyes rested on the portrait of her grandmother, Elizabeth Kelly, which was directly ahead, hanging on the wall over an imitation Ming vase.

"How perfect," she muttered. Just what she needed. The original Southern belle giving her the evil eye. How many times had she taken a "practice" walk down an imaginary runway over the years for her mother's and grandmother's amusement? It was impossible to count.

"Huh?" Michelle whispered, pacing herself next to Margo. "What's perfect?"

Margo shook her head. "Nothing, really." She

reached the wall and turned to Priscilla. "Well, how did we look?"

"Positively regal," Priscilla announced.

"You looked like a funeral procession," Vivienne cracked. "If everyone walked so slow, they'd need to hold auditions for a month instead of two days." She began snapping her fingers. "Step, step, step." She pulled a stopwatch from her jeans pocket. "Maybe we should use this."

Priscilla shook her head. "We don't need that. But actually, you're right. I was concentrating more on carriage."

"Well, they certainly held themselves straight," Gina remarked, standing up from her cross-legged position on the thick blue carpet. "But they didn't look as if they were having fun. You know. Loose." Gina moved across the room, taking long athletic strides. "You see, something like this. I mean, you're not going to be modeling clothes for a coronation or anything."

Margo giggled. "True, but I'm not supposed to be loping onto a baseball diamond, either!"

"Or chasing tennis balls," Michelle joined in.

"Wait a minute," Priscilla interjected, glancing at the stricken expression on Gina's face. "Gina had a good point. You have to walk tall and straight, of course. But you also have to look re-laxed. As if you're enjoying yourself."

"But, I'm not!" Margo cried out, laughing just the same. "I'm starving! It's been four days and

I can't stop thinking about grilled-cheese sandwiches and vanilla milk shakes."

"But, Margo, your stomach looks flatter already," Michelle insisted. "In another three days you're going to be thrilled."

Margo shrugged. Thrilled wasn't quite the right word.

Terrified was more like it.

Terrified that despite everything, she wouldn't be chosen. Terrified she'd be left with a broken heart and a mother who might never recover. Terrified that . . . Margo suddenly flashed on a vision of herself walking down the aisle. The same not-so-long legs, thick but unruly hair, and slightly trimmer, but not tiny, waist. Margo stayed with the vision for just a moment and suddenly shuddered. Actually, there was one thing more terrifying than not being chosen.

And that was being chosen. Being chosen and finding out that even that would not satisfy her mother. Or her. Margo could feel the tears begin to gather. Sooner or later Mrs. Warner was going to have to realize Margo was not her dream daughter. And Margo? Well, she was going to have to stop dreaming.

"Oh, Margo, Margo . . . " Michelle's voice persisted, interrupting Margo's dismal thoughts. "Come back, you look miserable."

"I was just thinking. . . . " Margo began. "I'm afraid. What if all this blows up and . . . "

"Is this the Ford modeling agency?" Mrs. Warner's voice suddenly rang out from the foyer. "I heard there's a group of gorgeous girls in here. Is that true?"

Margo rolled her eyes. "Mom! What are you doing home?!" She turned to Michelle. "Just what I need. You watch. She came home with a new diet food. Yesterday it was a magazine of new hairstyles. The day before that it was a book on dressing ten pounds thinner."

"Hello!" Mrs. Warner sang out as she entered the living room brandishing a foil bag. "Guess what's in here? Fat-free chocolate yogurt!"

"Sounds great," Gina replied.

"Mmmmmm," Michelle smiled, flashing Margo a sympathetic look.

"I'll take the fattening stuff, thanks," Vivienne grinned.

Margo turned slowly toward her mother. "Don't want any, thanks." Then she looked away. The truth was it sounded delicious. In fact, if she'd seen it herself, she'd have bought some.

But coming from her mother, it was just too much pressure.

Which was why she'd cancelled the beauty parlor appointment.

And started her own exercise regime. Too bad she couldn't get out of Tuesday's shopping expedition.

If she failed, she didn't want to have to answer to anyone.

Or more specifically, she didn't want to have to say "Mom, despite everything you did, I blew it."

"Well," Margo looked around the room. "I guess that's it for today. Meeting adjourned." She smiled tentatively at her mother.

The real beauty queen was home.

"So . . . Mimi," Alexa began, tossing her thick blonde hair back over her shoulders. "What do you think? Do I look like a model, or what?"

Slowly, she made her way into the kitchen decked out in a skimpy, skintight purple turtleneck dress with a chain belt draped around her hips.

"Honey, you look very snazzy," Mimi, the Crafts' housekeeper and Alexa's most trusted confidante, said, grinning from ear to ear. "But what happens when it's time to breathe? Do you take it off?"

Alexa laughed. "I'm breathing, Mimi. Trust me. I'm just very thin. My stomach is as flat as a pancake," she proclaimed, running her hand over it just to check.

"So I see," Mimi nodded, shaking her head. "But I sure hope that's not the best thing you can say about yo'self." She opened a cookbook and began sifting through the pages.

"What's that supposed to mean?" Alexa's eyes narrowed. Mimi could be great. Also a pain.

"I mean, sometimes I think you think how you look is all that counts, and I'm here to tell you, you got that wrong." Mimi slammed shut the cookbook, and smiled at Alexa sweetly. "That's all I mean."

"Looks are VERY important," Alexa insisted. "You've forgotten."

Mimi chuckled. "Honey, looks are still important. Even at my age." She paused, patting her hair into place. "Which is not that old. I'm just sayin', they aren't everythin'."

"You've forgotten what it's like to be a teenager," Alexa insisted.

"Teenagers are people, honey, and I can tell you I'm still one of *them*." Mimi shook her head somberly. "And no one, not my age or yours, can make it on looks alone."

Alexa frowned. "They help, though. . . . "

"Yes," Mimi nodded as she reached for Alexa's hand. "But, honey, you got a lot more goin' for you than just those golden glow looks of yours."

"Like what?" Alexa asked, abruptly turning away, suddenly embarrassed by her own uncertainty.

"Like your warm heart underneath all that meanness you think I don't know you shovel around every chance you get. Nibblin' at this person. Nibblin' at that. And you got more than a few brains up there in that head of yours if you'd just decide to take 'em out and give 'em some exercise. How's that for starters?"

Alexa shrugged.

"And you certainly got yo' friends goin'. The phone in this house never stops ringin' for you."

Suddenly, Alexa remembered Barry.

"Mimi, how come it's hard to talk to some people?"

Mimi reached for another cookbook. "Not everybody travels down the same river."

Alexa eyed Mimi warily. "Is that another one of your island sayings? I hate them. They're pretty, but they don't make sense."

Mimi chuckled. "It's one of my sayin's. And it means some people you'll have a natural flow with, and some you won't."

"Well, but what do you do about the ones you don't?"

"You act nice to them, and let them go their way while you go yours."

Alexa shook her head. "But what if you really LIKE one of those people who . . . who . . . are traveling down a different river?"

Mimi laughed. "You want to know what to do if you really like someone you can't talk to?" She paused. "I'd work at it a little bit. See if that person was real shy, or if I just needed to find somethin' we could share. And if it still didn't click, I'd ask myself why I want to be with this person anyway. Chances are I wouldn't come up with much of a reason."

"But he's so cute," Alexa protested.

"See what I mean?" Mimi replied quietly.

7

"How's Gina doing?" Margo whispered. She looked into the pool, but it was impossible to tell who was who with all the splashing water and bobbing heads in white caps.

"Good," Vivienne replied. "But I cannot stand the smell of chlorine."

Margo nodded. It was a little overpowering. She leaned against a tiled wall and studied Sandy, the swimming coach.

"Don't drop off, Walters!" he called out sternly. "Keep moving, Dumont. Those kicks are disappearing. Let's MOVE!"

Margo shook her head. He was impossible. Gina complained about him all the time.

A moment later, he blew his whistle. "Okay! That's enough for today. Get a good night's sleep." He chuckled. "See you here the day after tomorrow."

Margo grabbed a towel and moved to the edge of the pool. Gina pulled herself out and reached for it with a big smile.

"Thanks," she said, slightly out of breath. She wrapped herself up in the towel. "I hate Sandy. I really do."

Margo nodded understandingly. It was the same with her mother. Always pushing for more.

"He's so tough," Gina continued. "I don't know what he expects."

"I know just what you mean," Margo began. "I mean, when my mother . . . "

"It's okay, though," Gina continued, now suddenly laughing.

Margo looked at her with surprise. "I thought you just said you can't stand him."

"I can't," Gina replied with a shrug. "But he's going to make us into a winning team. I just know it. Besides," she paused, "I can tell he thinks I could be very good. I like that."

"You're the best," Vivienne interrupted as she handed Gina a brush. "Now go change. We gotta get out of here before I start smelling like Esther Williams."

Gina looked at her curiously. "Who?"

Vivienne shook her head. "Forget it. She's a swimming star in those old movies I like to watch."

Gina nodded and headed off in the direction of the locker rooms.

"So. What's the matter with you?" Vivienne asked, eyeing Margo suspiciously. "You look sick."

Margo shrugged as she headed for the double doors leading away from the pool. "I guess I was just thinking about my mother."

"What about her?"

"The fact that every day she keeps pushing. 'What did you eat today?' 'Can I help you practice walking?' 'Would you like to see the pictures of me in the pageant?' It's driving me crazy. And tonight she's taking me shopping for the first tryouts."

Vivienne shook her head. "Look, the modeling thing will all be over in ten days. You've got to stop thinking about it every minute!"

"I wasn't thinking about it just now," Margo insisted. "But Gina started talking about Sandy and how much she hates the way he pushes her, and then the next thing I see is she loves it, and I was just . . . "

"You were just wondering how come Gina doesn't mind being pushed, but you do?"

Margo nodded as she walked out into the fresh air. "I can't stand indoor pools."

"Don't change the subject," Vivienne commented lightly. "And if you want an answer, here it is. I think it's because Gina really wants to be a swimmer. She's a natural athlete."

"Right," Margo commented dryly. "And I am not a natural beauty."

"I didn't say that," Vivienne snapped. "What I meant is that I think you want to be more than just pretty. Boy, are you sensitive these days. It's really getting on my nerves. . . . "

Margo shrugged. "Sue me." She looked up at the sky for a long moment.

"Hi, guys!" Gina called out, bursting through the doors. "Was that quick enough? Thanks for waiting."

"You looked good out there," Margo offered, trying to sound cheerful.

Gina grimaced. "I didn't feel so good. I think I'm slipping or something."

"Ridiculous," Vivienne proclaimed.

"Well, my parents pointed out I haven't been spending as much . . . "

"Your parents are too hard on you," Margo protested. "They make me angry."

"Yes, well, you know what that feels like, huh?" Gina commented, flashing Margo a sad smile."

"But you drive yourself so hard." Margo touched her shoulder lightly. "It must not be a lot of fun."

"Well . . . " Gina sighed thoughtfully. "It isn't. But . . . " She stopped and looked at Margo carefully. "Sometimes going after what you really want isn't fun."

Margo hesitated. Actually, that was true.

"The thing is, you have to figure out what's really important to you," Gina continued. "Because once you know, it keeps you going." She sighed. "At least that's what Sandy always says."

Margo nodded.

Now there was an interesting point. Lately everything had gotten so heated up, it was hard to tell who wanted what and how much.

She shook her head with bewilderment.

It didn't much matter now.

What had Sandy called out?

Right. "LET'S MOVE!"

Well, that's what she was doing.

In her way, she was swimming just as fast as she could.

"How about this one, sweetheart?"

Margo lifted her eyes to the dressing room mirror Tuesday evening and shuddered. Where was her mother finding these things?

"It looks like a strawberry parfait," Margo mumbled. "I am not trying out for dessert of the month."

Mrs. Warner looked at her daughter and then at the dress with surprise. "What are you talking about, dear? This is precisely the sort of thing that shows a girl off to her best advantage. Just look at it!" She ran her hand lovingly over the satin bodice.

Margo turned to study the bright-pink, puff-sleeved, sweetheart-necked, rose-at-the-hip, semiformal misery. Sighing heavily, she shook her head. "You're on the wrong track, Mother. Trust me."

Mrs. Warner glanced at the short, simple navy blue V-necked dress Margo was now wearing. "Not the right color for you, dear. It's draining."

Margo glanced at herself in the mirror. Actually, she'd thought she looked good. Margo cocked her head to one side. Well, she was partly right. Her body did look good. But something was definitely wrong. The color did leave her looking sort of . . . tired. Once again she sighed, and then checked her watch.

Half an hour left to this Tuesday night outing. What a relief. Kind of. She still hadn't found an outfit. Margo eyed the discarded clothes that lay in a jumble on a chair in the corner of the dressing room. "I liked that sweater." She pointed to a green sweater that lay almost at the bottom of the pile. It had a nice sleek line, and the V-neck showed off her longish neck.

Mrs. Warner smiled. "Well, you can't just wear that!" She started laughing way too uproariously. Margo wanted to slap her.

"I'm going to put my clothes back on and see if I can find something to go with it," Margo declared. "I felt good in that."

"It's nice for school, dear, but a fashion show?" Mrs. Warner commented softly as she watched Margo climb into her jeans. "Isn't it a little . . . well . . . casual?"

"I think it's stylish," Margo insisted, not at all sure this was so. Desperately, she wished she'd brought someone from the Crowd along. And that her mother had stayed home.

"I do think you should listen to me on this," Mrs. Warner plowed on. "I mean, I do have experience with . . . "

"THIS IS NOT A BEAUTY PAGEANT," Margo practically hissed. "This is a fashion show for teen fashion. This sweater is a teen fashion. I am a teen. Okay? Stop it!"

"I do not like your tone of voice this evening." Mrs. Warner's mood turned abruptly dark. "I have been very patient with you. I am trying to help. To give you the benefit of my experience."

Margo nodded quickly. "I'm sorry. I know you're trying to help. I'm just tense." She looked away. This was exhausting.

Mrs. Warner flashed her daughter a bright, forgiving smile. "I understand. Who else can you snap at but your mother?!"

Margo nodded again. "Yes, who else?" she responded softly. She turned, pushed aside the curtains, and walked out onto the floor.

Immediately to her right Margo spotted a white mid-calf wool skirt. Too dressy. To her left she eyed a pair of black corduroy slacks with a yoke front. Too slim-cut. Straight ahead a row of bright-red pleated skirts dangled invitingly. Cute, but no good. Matched with the green sweater, she'd look like a Christmas tree.

Margo walked to the front of the teen fashion

department in Gerrards and surveyed the racks. There had to be something. She had half an hour. All she needed was something simple. Something slimming. Something eye-catching. Something flattering.

How hard could that be? Margo ran a hand over her almost flat stomach and felt as if she wanted to cry.

"We'll find it!" Mrs. Warner's voice whispered.

Margo looked up to find her mother standing beside her, eagerly eyeing the racks of clothes. She held up the green sweater. "There must be something here that will give this just the right look. . . ."

Margo nodded hopefully. Unbelievable. Her mother was starting to get it.

"Why, look at this!" Mrs. Warner called out, racing over to a white and light-blue cotton sweater with embroidered pastel flowers along the sleeves and scoop neckline. "And this!" She yanked out a knee-length soft-blue shirt. The green sweater was now draped over Mrs. Warner's shoulder like a damp dishrag, completely forgotten.

Margo nodded. "Nice." Then she turned and started looking through the racks diagonally to her right. Nice and horrible. Nice and not her. Nice and Southern belle-ish.

"It's not me," Margo called over her shoulder,

not daring to look at her mother. "Please put it back."

Margo heard the gentle "ting" of wire hitting rack.

Good.

She checked her watch. Twenty minutes to go.

How many more horrendous items could her mother possibly find?

"Margo! Look at this!" Mrs. Warner's voice rang across the floor moments later.

Margo checked her watch. Nineteen minutes.

She turned around.

Actually, the dress was lovely.

If you didn't mind looking like Tinkerbell.

8

"Okay? Alexa asked Robin, knowing full well it certainly was. She looked more than okay. She looked great.

"Really beautiful," Robin nodded. "You'll get a spot. I just know it."

"Mmmmm," Alexa replied dreamily. "And wait till Barry sees me. If the sight of me in the show doesn't get him going, I don't know what will!" Once again she glanced at the phone, still hoping he'd call to wish her luck. He'd certainly sounded impressed when she'd told him about Gerrards. In fact, he'd even said he was going to tell his buddies.

"Where did you get that incredible dress?" Robin asked, reaching out to touch the snug, aqua-blue cotton lycra scoop-necked dress. "And that chain belt?"

Alexa smiled. "At Gerrards. Where else? I thought it was a good idea to let them see how good their clothes look on me. . . . " She ran her fingers over the gold links that were resting along her hips. "This was a gift from my mom. It was even too expensive for my clothes allowance. She was in a rush the other day, and I said, 'Before you go, could you just get me one special thing for the modeling tryouts?' And POW! There it was. Mucho money."

"Your mom is really great," Robin sighed.

"Yeah," Alexa nodded, quickly looking away. Everyone thought that. It was amazing. Hardly anyone ever saw her, but they still thought she was terrific. Ah, well. Maybe she was.

"Well, here I go." Alexa twirled around once, just as the phone began to ring.

"Hello?"

"Alexa?"

"Barry!" It was hard to believe. He'd remembered. "Is this a good-luck call?"

"No, and well, yes it is," a familiar voice rang across the wire. "It isn't Barry, but I am calling to wish you good luck. Modeling is a little mindless, but you're not."

"Excuse me?" Alexa asked, completely confused. It was David. And it seemed as if he'd just insulted her, but not quite. "What did you say?"

David chuckled. "Barry told me about your tryouts today. He got caught up with the swim team, and I asked him if he minded if I called to wish you good luck."

"Oh . . . " Alexa replied slowly. "And he said?" Not at all sure what she wanted to hear.

"He said fine, but that I should try and contain my charm."

"He did?!" Alexa exclaimed. "That's very nice!" She glanced in the mirror. It was finally happening. She had started to get to him. "What else did he say?"

"Nothing," David answered. He paused. "You must be nervous."

Alexa thought about that for a minute. Nerves didn't suit her image very well. "A little," she offered casually.

"You'll be great," David responded quickly. "Everyone gets nervous when they have to perform. Speaking of which, I've got to run. I'm about to shoot some hoops with the guys."

"Oh, okay," Alexa answered quickly. "Thanks for calling."

"Sure," David answered. And a moment later he was gone.

Alexa slowly hung up the phone. Things were looking good. Really good. Yes, sir.

"What did Barry say?" Robin asked enthusiastically.

"That wasn't Barry. It was David," Alexa replied.

"David? But where was Barry?"

"At swim practice."

"So what did David want?"

"To wish me good luck," Alexa replied, suddenly feeling just a little less terrific.

"You mean, to tell you Barry wished you good luck?"

"Not exactly," Alexa shrugged. The good feeling was definitely ebbing.

"You mean David called to wish you good luck, but Barry didn't?" Robin blurted out. "Isn't that weird?"

"No, it isn't," Alexa snapped. "He was just being friendly, and Barry was busy."

"Well, where was David?"

"Playing basketball."

"That's busy, too," Robin barrelled on.

"Enough!" Alexa finally cried out. What was with Robin today, anyway? Just when she needed a yes-man, Robin was turning into a criminal attorney.

"Okay," Robin quickly replied. "I was just surprised. I mean, look, Barry was busy, and David just wanted . . . "

"I don't need a summary," Alexa interrupted irritably. "I just told YOU what happened."

"Of course you did," Robin assured her.

Alexa looked away. Yes, she certainly knew what had happened.

What she didn't know was what it meant.

It was hard to believe the week was over.

Margo studied her reflection in the mirror for a long moment.

Those few pounds had made a difference. Her

hair was shiny. Her eyes looked large and bright. She smiled. Her face lit up nicely.

Margo took a step closer to the mirror and studied a spot on her chin. No. It wasn't going to be a pimple. She stepped back once more and looked at her knees. Not too pudgy. Not too . . .

Margo stopped abruptly. Enough. She was making herself sick.

She turned to study Michelle, who was now leaning into the small makeup mirror on Margo's desk and carefully applying black mascara.

"You look beautiful," Margo offered as her eyes traveled over Michelle's slim figure, which was now tucked neatly into a narrow red skirt and white V-necked pullover. She looked away. Michelle would have made a terrific Kelly girl.

Michelle looked up. "Would you believe it if I said the same thing to you?"

Margo smiled shyly. "Well, you could tell me I look good. I think I might believe that."

"Well," Michelle grinned, "you look . . . terrific." She started laughing at the look on Margo's face. "I know it's tough to hear, but give it a try!"

Margo glanced back in the mirror. The long emerald-green sweater she wore flattered her coloring, and the line it created over the pleated black skirt that ended two inches above her knees gave her a long, if not exactly slim, look.

She could feel the excitement inside her beginning to mount.

"I am the modeling type," she whispered, speaking the words slowly. Trying them on for size.

Michelle grinned. "Thatta girl."

Margo stood up. "What were those odds again? Vivienne said she heard how many girls were applying for how many spots?"

"Approximately one hundred girls for twenty spots. That's one-in-five odds," Michelle reported. "That's why they had to split the first part of the auditions into two groups."

"Not great," Margo sighed. She bent down and gave herself one more lingering look in the makeup mirror. She closed her eyes for just a moment.

If only this didn't mean so much.

Michelle tucked her arm through Margo's. "Let's go, beautiful. Forget about your mother. Just think about you."

Margo squared her shoulders. "I'm ready. Or as ready as I'll ever . . . "

"Oh, Margo!" Mrs. Warner's voice rang up the stairs as the front door closed behind her. "I rushed out of work early to take a look!" A second later she bounded into Margo's room.

"How lovely you look!" she exclaimed. Then she tilted her head to one side. "I do wish you'd kept that hair appointment with Jaré, though, dear. It could use a little shaping." She reached into her bag and pulled out a brush.

Quickly, Margo backed away. "No, thanks," she insisted. She shot Michelle a warning glance. "We're late. Michelle will fix my hair when we get there." She began edging for the door.

"Oh, honey, I want to help. . . . " Mrs Warner implored. "You both look so lovely, and you know I have lots of experience with . . . "

Margo couldn't decide if she wanted to smack or kiss her mother. The last thing she needed to think about now was Mrs. Warner's beauty career.

Wordlessly, she turned and headed for the stairs.

"Well, alright, dear," Mrs. Warner called out after her. "I know you're nervous. I was just trying to fix that frizz. . . . "

"I'll get to it later," Margo called back. "I promise."

Her hand reached up self-consciously to the problem spot. Her hair always frizzed in the back on the right side, just a little.

She couldn't help it. Her mother couldn't tame it. And Jaré, in the end, would have changed nothing.

It was just her. Margo Warner. Imperfect in many ways.

Still, wasn't she, at least today, just maybe pretty enough? Margo frowned.

Apparently not.

9

Margo looked around the large waiting room and instantly wanted to go home. Not that everyone was so pretty. Not everyone was. It was the way everyone was staring at each other.

Scoring each other.

Weighing each other.

Trying to decide if this one with the long dark bangs and high cheekbones, or that one with the thick eyelashes and sunlit hair, could steal her spot.

Margo studied her shoes. The truth was they all had a better shot than she did. Why torture herself?

"Look," Michelle whispered, pointing to an empty corner of the room. "Let's wait there." She looked around. "Oh, hi, Pamela!" she called out. She began to chuckle. "Funny how nobody from school wanted to admit they were doing this, and I've already spotted at least five other girls from our class!"

"Hysterical," Margo replied dryly. Michelle was

65

getting on her nerves. She straightened the pleats on her skirt self-consciously. Michelle was pretty sure she'd be chosen. People who were sure they wouldn't were not about to announce they were trying.

Suddenly, the door to Ms. Pik's office flew open, and the director of the fashion show stepped out. A tall, slim woman with stylish blunt-cut dark hair, she was dressed in a pale-pink wool suit and softly striped shirt.

"I presume all of you have filled out the forms my assistant passed out and that you've turned them in either here or at school."

A soft chorus of yesses filled the room.

"Alright, then," she continued with a big smile, "here is how it's going to work. Your names will be called out one at a time. You'll walk in, smile for me, answer a few questions about your schedule, turn around once or twice, and exit." Ms. Pik clasped her hands together under her chin. "After I've seen each of you, I'll ask you to wait a little bit and then I'll come back out and announce the names of those girls I'd like to see again on Friday. I'll do the same with the group of girls I see tomorrow." She looked around the room with a kind smile. "I just want to say you all look lovely. Mine is going to be a very difficult job." And with that, she turned around, walked into her office, and closed the door.

Margo turned to Michelle and smiled uncomfortably. The truth was, she felt very bizarre. Kind of like a zebra in a forest. Or an owl in a palm tree. Margo smiled to herself. This was fun. Putting things in places they didn't quite belong. It was a good game.

She looked around the room. This, however, was not.

Absentmindedly, she turned to her left and found herself gazing at a tall dark-haired girl she'd never seen before.

At first glance, she was awfully pretty. A second glance, however, brought other news. She was wearing too much makeup, her hair was all in place but sticky with mousse, and her dress was very glitzy but not particularly elegant. The whole look screamed, "I GOTTA BE SOMEONE PRETTY. I JUST GOTTA!" Margo looked down at her own simple outfit. What did it say? Margo pondered the question for a moment.

Finally, she nudged Michelle. "What's •my look?" she whispered.

"Huh?" Michelle responded.

"What does my look say?" Margo persisted. "You know. Like it might say, 'I'm a simple person,' or 'I want to be a lawyer.'"

Michelle giggled. "Oh. I see." She turned and studied Margo. "I'd say your look says, 'I'm straightforward. I like to be natural.'"

Margo nodded, a little disappointed. It didn't sound like a winning portrait. Still, it was honest. She had tried to look like herself. But prettier. And thinner.

Suddenly, she thought of the bake sale, and the organization her class had chosen. The Port Andrews Committee for the Homeless.

And then she flashed on her mother. Her warm, well-meaning, pushy mother. Margo began nervously fingering the straps of her shoulder bag.

"Jill Plow," Ms. Pik's assistant, Pamela, called out. The girl to Margo's left moved forward.

"Good luck," Margo whispered, meaning it sincerely. She looked like a girl who HAD to make it. She looked like someone who would fall apart if she didn't. She looked like someone who made looks her number-one priority.

But, most of all, she looked like someone Margo had no desire to be.

Margo shook her head ever so slightly. It was so confusing. She ached to be the most beautiful girl in the world. But there were other things that meant a lot to Margo, too. Unlike her mother. Or so it seemed.

Margo sighed. It was so hard to know who was really in charge of her life. Who really knew what was right for Margo.

Always, there seemed to be two voices, her

mother's and hers, urging her on. In two different directions.

Most times she could follow her own very special way. But not when Mrs. Warner tapped into her secret dreams. Not when she ached for the same things as Margo. Then the line became hazy.

And scary. Because then, when Margo lost, Mrs. Warner lost, too. It was just too much responsibility.

"Margo Warner," Pamela called out.

"Go get 'em," Michelle whispered encouragingly.

As if in a fog, Margo stood up and began walking forward. If only her mother hadn't known. If only her mother hadn't seen into that perplexing space where Margo's dreams and her own melted into one and the same. If only they both hadn't wanted Margo to be the belle of the ball, the queen of the pageant, the most beautiful girl in the world.

If only her mother had let her be, Margo would have been safely at home, talking with friends, and planning the bake sale, instead of fighting for a dream she had no business chasing.

Darn her mother.

Margo held her head high as she stepped into Ms. Pik's office.

"Hello," Ms. Pik offered casually. "Please come in and walk toward me."

For a moment, she hesitated. "Go ahead," a voice inside her head implored. "You can do it. You want it so much. Try."

Margo smiled falteringly.

"Now!" the voice insisted.

Margo stepped forward.

The voice was right. And though it was hard to admit, it had been her own.

10

Alexa walked out of Gerrards onto the sun-washed sidewalk and headed for the bus stop. She began to smile.

Success. It was a beautiful thing.

She caught a glimpse of herself in a store window and casually shook her hair back over her shoulders. A natural beauty. That's what she was. Ms. Pik had simply confirmed the fact.

Yes, congratulations were in order.

Almost instantly, Alexa's smile began to fade. But from whom?

Anxiously, Alexa began to chew on the inside of her cheek.

Mona. It would be nice to hear a congratulations from Mona. Also Barry. It would be spectacular to hear it from him.

Alexa reached the bus stop. Lost in thought, she mounted the steps and took a seat. She looked up at the bus route that was posted along the opposite wall. Mona's stop was two before hers. She smiled. Surely this news would break the ice between them. Sure, they'd had a scene. They always had scenes. That was their way. Or rather her way.

Small difference.

"Hello, Alexa," Mrs. Davis smiled wanly as she opened the door. "Mona is upstairs."

Alexa nodded, suddenly a littly sorry she had come. Mona's was not the happiest house. Her father was often out of work, her mother was usually in a bad mood, and Mona didn't act like herself when she was there.

For some reason, Alexa usually didn't mind, though. Mostly she just felt badly for Mona. That was something important between them. Mona knew she didn't have to put on a show. Or hide things. In fact, though Alexa opted not to tell her so, she often found Mona's house interesting. If not a relief. Nobody even pretended to be happy. Alexa often had the feeling that her own home life was nothing but another one of her mother's TV commercials. Or maybe only *she* was acting. . . . It was hard to tell.

Alexa sprinted up the stairs and knocked on Mona's door.

"Come in," she heard her friend call out.

"Hi," Alexa said as she opened the door and smiled at Mona.

Mona looked up with a blank expression.

For a moment, Alexa almost turned around. But something made her stand her ground. She'd come for congratulations. She wasn't leaving without them.

"I made callbacks," Alexa said simply. Surely Mona would see this was a time to drop past grudges. Good news did that to people.

"Congratulations," Mona smiled. "I am glad for you. You wanted it a lot. I know that."

"Thanks!" Alexa said brightly, trying to pretend she was getting exactly what she'd come for, which wasn't even slightly true. This just was not like Mona. She didn't yes Alexa to death like Robin. But she sure did like to avoid a fight.

Mona just stared at her.

"What's the matter?"

"I don't like the way you snap at me," Mona replied quietly. "I really don't."

Alexa sat down. She didn't like the sound of that at all. Mona was supposed to understand her "way."

Besides, all she'd come for was congratulations.

"I ran into Barry today," Mona went on, changing the subject.

"Oh, yeah?" Alexa replied uncertainly.

"Yes, he helped me with the debate thing."

"He's smart," Alexa nodded. She was starting to get an uncomfortable feeling.

"He's going to help me again, I think," Mona

continued, standing up to look out the window. "Nothing's happened, though."

"What do you mean?" Alexa asked, not at all sure she wanted to catch Mona's drift.

"Nothing," Mona continued. "That's just it. I wanted you to know that in case someone told you they saw us together. It's totally innocent. You just have a habit of going nuts over stuff like that. . . ."

"He's my boyfriend," Alexa replied, intending to say so with a bold voice. It came out as a whisper.

Mona shrugged.

"Why did you do that?" Alexa asked sharply.

"I needed the help," Mona replied.

"No, I mean shrug. Why did you shrug?"

Mona sighed heavily. "I don't know. I guess I don't think you guys are right for each other."

"Oh. And how would you know? You're never around. You never see us together!" Alexa sputtered. "And anyway, who is right for him? You?"

"No!" Mona cried out. "You're doing it again. Just forget it, okay? And by the way, the other day when I told you I needed your help, I meant it. You're smarter than you think about a lot of things."

"Not when it comes to friends," Alexa snapped.

"Please don't say that," Mona implored.

"Okay. Well, then, I'll just think it," Alexa responded. She turned and walked out of the room.

Racing down the stairs, Alexa flew out of the front door and into the street.

The tears began to spill over her cheeks.

It wasn't right. It wasn't fair.

What was Mona really saying?

Maybe she should have stayed. Asked more questions. Sorted it all out. Mona was worth at least that.

No. It just wasn't her way.

Alexa began to run.

From something. She just wasn't sure what.

"Margo, I'm so proud of you!" Mrs. Warner practically shrieked. "You see! You've got it! You've got the Kelly magic!"

"I didn't get a spot yet," Margo grinned. "I just made callbacks." The words still felt unreal. There she'd sat, waiting for the names to be called, positive that hers would not be among them, and yet there it had been! Michelle's, too. It was simply too exciting for words.

"That Kelly magic does it every time," Mrs. Warner proclaimed.

Margo smiled a bit less enthusiastically this time. Kelly this. Kelly that. Why wasn't it ever "Margo magic"? Something different. Something of her making. An image all her own. Whether she got a spot or not, she'd still never be Miss Georgia Peach material. Never. Couldn't her mother see that?

"You'll see. They'll call your name on Friday. I know they will. Goodness, I have to call my friends and tell them the good news."

"Please don't," Margo cried out. "Please. I may not make it. You're going to feel terrible then. . . . "

"Oh, don't worry," Mrs. Warner assured her. "I'll tell them it's not over till it's over. Trust me!" And with that, she sailed out of the kitchen into the den where Margo could hear her excitedly picking up the phone.

Margo smiled after her ruefully. If only she had her mother's confidence. She walked through the hallway and into the guest powder room. She gazed at herself for a long moment.

Actually, she did look pretty.

She could hear her name being called out now. "Margo Warner." "Margo Warner." "Margo Warner."

She studied her face. Was it possible she was REALLY good looking? Great looking, in fact? Prettier than most?

What a splendid thing that would be.

It certainly seemed possible. After all. They'd called her name. "Margo Warner!"

And not because she'd won an election, or started a committee, or told a good joke.

No. They'd called her name because of her looks.

What an absolute, impossible thrill.

Margo sailed out of the powder room and up the stairs to her bedroom, a curious feeling of surprise beginning to descend.

It was an odd thought that began to take form. Almost insulting, really. But not quite. Actually, it was kind of humorous.

Who would have believed that she, Margo Warner, could be so incredibly superficial?

11

Thursday morning, Margo woke up feeling beautiful.

Dressing carefully in blue-denim culottes and a long-sleeved black T-shirt, she ran a comb through what she now considered to be her magnificent thick curls and walked downstairs.

Lewis was in the kitchen pouring himself some cereal.

"Hello, brother dear," Margo sang out. "And how are you this morning?"

"Fine, skinny. How about you?" he asked, flashing her a smile. "Heard about your triumph yesterday. Man, I think you'll never get rid of Mom now." He started laughing. "You Kelly girl, you."

Margo grabbed an apple and took a bite. It was true. It wasn't good. She shrugged. "Well, who knows? Maybe she'll lighten up. Right now, I'm just worried about tomorrow."

Lewis shrugged. "You surprise me. I didn't know you cared about stuff like modeling. . . . "

"You mean you didn't know I cared about my

looks?" Margo replied defensively. "I look like I don't care about my looks?"

"No," Lewis replied, laughing. "Calm down! It's not that. You just always seemed like you were interested in other things more. You know. Like student affairs and politics." He paused. "Whatever."

"I still am," Margo answered, again defensively. She quickly checked in her knapsack for the address of the chairman of the Committee for the Homeless. She was due there directly after school to discuss where the money from the bake sale would go.

Guiltily, she stared at the blank pad in her bag. She should have planned for this meeting. Made lists of projects her class wanted to back. Worked out some ideas for how the class could continue to help even after the bake sale was over.

Of course, if she got to school early she could probably get it all written up by lunchtime.

"Gotta run," Margo muttered. Throwing her knapsack over her shoulder, Margo threw a quick good-bye in her brother's direction and headed toward the door.

She stole a glance in the mirror. That frizzy spot was sticking out all over the place. Ducking into the bathroom, she grabbed her brush, wet it down, and ran it through her hair. It still wasn't right. She dashed upstairs, found a blow dryer, and worked on the spot a bit longer.

Finally, it was under control.

Satisfied, Margo bolted down the stairs and out the door. She smiled and held her face up to the sun. She felt different. A good different. She wondered if anyone would notice. The new, the improved, the truly good-looking Margo Warner.

Margo began to sing as she made her way down the street.

"A pretty girl, ta da da da, is like a melody . . . "

Who used to sing that song? Ah, yes. Margo smiled sadly. Her father. Years ago . . .

Who had he sung it to, though? Her mother — or her?

Suddenly Margo was bursting with the desire to know one thing.

Could he see her now? And if the answer was yes, did he think she was pretty?

She felt tears spring to her eyes.

Didn't all fathers think their daughters were beautiful?

Probably.

Margo began looking through her knapsack for a tissue.

Suddenly, she missed her father almost more than she could bear. . . .

"Great news, Alexa!" Julie called out over everyone's head as Alexa walked into the lunchroom.

Alexa nodded with a big smile. "Haven't got it yet!" she called out modestly. Julie waved it away as if to say, "Don't be silly." Alexa nodded again. Julie was right, of course. She was star material. Her eyes rested on Michelle Horne and Margo Warner as they sat giggling softly together. Alexa smiled. Did they really think that just because they made callbacks they could hold a candle to her?

She looked quickly around the lunchroom for Robin. Her eyes settled on James Wood. What a puppy dog. Now there was someone who thought everything she said, every move she made, every toss of her head was just . . . well . . . perfection. Alexa smiled at the thought. Then she spotted Mona, who was sitting alone reading a book. She waited for the anger to surge forward. There she was. Her supposed best friend, acting as if she had never betrayed a soul. How phony, Alexa muttered to herself. How enraging. How . . .

It was a curious thing. Alexa wondered if she was losing it altogether. The truth was, she didn't feel that angry.

What she felt was something else.

Like embarrassed, for instance.

For a brief moment, Alexa considered walking over and trying to clear the air. After all, Mona had been, when it came right down to it, very honest. Painfully honest, in fact.

A little touch of anger kicked in. Actually, who

does she think she is, deciding who really likes whom? What did she really know about how people REALLY feel inside? Or about how important Barry had become to her. For whatever reason.

Alexa looked away. No. Let her sit by herself for a while. "Alexa!" Pete Stimmel called out. Alexa turned around with a big smile. Just the other day she'd noticed he'd gotten very cute. Tall. Kind of rugged. She was about to walk over to his table when she noticed a figure through the glass windows of the cafeteria beckoning to her. Stepping forward, she realized it was David Parker. Hesitating, she put her tray down on the nearest table and slid open the glass door. Maybe he had a message from Barry, who hadn't even called last night.

"Hi, Alexa!" he called out, walking toward her.

Alexa smiled slightly at the tall slim figure that was fast approaching. She didn't want to lead him on. He was cute. His sandy curly hair looked very California-ish. But he was no Barry, that was for sure. He didn't have that . . . magic.

"Heard you made it." He began patting Alexa's cheek ever so lightly. "Barry told me. You must feel great." He paused. "Though I'm not sure why. You already know you're good-looking and . . . " Suddenly, he stopped, looked into her eyes, and started chuckling.

"What's so funny?" Alexa muttered, looking around to see if she could spot Barry. If Barry knew she'd done it, why hadn't he called last night? And who told him, anyway?

Mona?

Alexa felt a pinch of anger again.

"You don't know for sure you're good-looking . . . do you!?" David answered. "You need proof!"

Alexa looked at him wide-eyed. Who did he think he was, anyway? Freud?

"Don't bother denying it." David shook his head. "I wouldn't believe you."

"And I suppose you think you're some kind of Adonis," Alexa replied dryly. She looked him over from head to toe. Actually, he wasn't half bad. Not her type, though. He didn't have that star quality she so loved. . . .

"Actually, no, I don't," David replied somberly. "But I think I have charisma." He folded both arms across his chest with confidence. "Yup. I think I've got what it takes."

"What takes?" Alexa asked, chuckling in spite of herself. He was really rather charming. He'd make someone a very nice boyfriend.

"What it takes to go out with you," David replied.

For a moment, Alexa was stunned. Not that she didn't sense he liked her. That was old news. But that he said so. Just like that. No pretense. No beating around the bush.

Actually, it was kind of cute.

Yes, he would definitely make someone a very nice boyfriend.

Alexa smiled. "You're such a joker," she replied. "Speaking of Barry, where is he?"

David shrugged. "I think he's in the library. He's all caught up in his science project. You know how he gets. . . . "

Alexa grinned. "I guess that's why he didn't call last night." She paused. "He's very smart."

David grinned broadly. "You think he didn't call last night because he's smart?"

Alexa could feel herself turning red. "How come you twist everything I say?"

David shrugged. "Maybe because a lot of things you say are twisted!" He reached forward again and touched her cheek. "Think about that, why don't you."

And with that, he turned around and walked back toward the high school.

"You think you're so smart," Alexa muttered under her breath, watching him walk away. Then she sighed.

He was smart.

She wasn't fooling him for a minute.

It was a unique experience.

Margo checked the number on the house one more time and then rang the bell. "Let's not make any jokes or anything," she urged Vivienne. "Mr.

Fox sounds like a very serious person on the phone."

Vivienne nodded somberly. "Well, you'd probably be serious, too, if you spent your days worrying about people who didn't have any homes."

Margo nodded guiltily, turning her eyes from the glass side panels of the front door in which she'd caught her reflection. No, she certainly hadn't spent much time worrying about homeless people. She had, however, spent a lot of time worrying about whether she was homely.

Margo smiled. Nice word play. Still, she felt ever so slightly pathetic.

"Hello, girls." The door suddenly flew open to reveal a youngish man with thinning hair, warm brown eyes, and a friendly smile. "Good to meet you. I'm Robert Fox. But my friends call me Bob."

"Hello," Margo began. "I'm Margo Warner, and this is my co-chairman, Vivienne Bennis." She paused. "We know you're busy, but we just wanted to talk with you about the proceeds from our bake sale and also whatever else our class can do for you."

"Thrilled to hear it," Bob replied with a broad grin. A moment later a more somber look crept over his face. "Ours is not an easy task. There are desperate people out there."

Vivienne nodded. "We know. My parents talk about it all the time, and the news . . . "

Bob shook his head vigorously. "The news doesn't show the half of it."

"Well, that's what our teacher says," Margo nodded. "And that's why we chose this committee." She reached into her bag for her notes.

Bob started walking into the main room of the house, which had been converted into a giant office. "Please sit down!" He nodded toward a young woman on the phone. "That's Mindy. My assistant."

Margo waved in her direction and then took a seat in one of the comfortable easy chairs arranged in the center of the room. "I was wondering if I could tell you the things the class is interested in knowing about. We had some ideas of where we'd like this money to go and we were hoping we could influence . . . "

"Yes and no," Bob replied quickly. "It's often difficult to work that way. But we could try to direct at least some of the money you hand us into the right area. What did you have in mind?"

Wordlessly, Margo handed him a sheet of paper upon which she had typed the particular concerns of the class, as well as her own ideas of what they might do to serve the nearby homeless community. Especially the children.

Bob considered the paper silently for a moment.

"We're open to any of your suggestions, of course," Vivienne interjected. "We know we can't possible understand or be aware of all the problems. . . . "

"Did you draw up this proposal?" Bob asked, eyeing Margo.

Margo twisted uncomfortably in her seat. "Yes, I did. But, of course, I know I'm probably naive about what really needs to be done. . . . "

"Not at all," Bob replied warmly. "This shows a very real feeling for the plight of these people." He looked at Margo for a moment. "I'm impressed. Offering to tutor children of this or nearby towns who are too distressed to concentrate in school is a sympathetic, useful idea."

Margo felt herself blush under his gaze. She looked away. She was proud of herself. She'd led the class well on this issue. She'd put the list together in a rush, but it still had heart. Happily, Margo turned to Vivienne and gave way to a soft smile.

She felt great. Comfortable. Like a zebra on a wide open African plain. Or an owl in a lush green forest tree.

Now where had she played that game before? Ah, yes. At the tryouts. Only then, everything had been out of place. Foreign. Awkward. Margo frowned, suddenly aware that she was more relaxed now than she'd been in days. Still . . .

Suddenly, she straightened her back and ran a hand through her hair. The new Margo Warner was not just a leader. She belonged in the world of beauty.

She smiled at Bob. Could he see that? Could he tell?

Probably not.

He was too busy. Too concerned with other things.

Margo sighed. Life had been a lot easier when she had been, too.

12

Alexa gazed around the waiting room outside Ms. Pik's office and allowed a contented sigh. There was competition, alright. But it wasn't stiff. She turned around slightly to take a better look at Michelle. It figured she'd wear royal blue today. It was her best color.

Alexa could feel the anger begin to surge. What was Michelle doing here, anyway? This wasn't her kind of thing. It couldn't possibly matter that much to her. Then her eyes traveled to Margo.

Alexa studied her for a long moment. Actually, she really was kind of pretty in a wholesome sort of way. But her body. Not the modeling type at all. Certainly not like Alexa's trim, curvy shape.

Alexa began to silently count the girls she thought were especially good-looking. It came to eight. She smiled. Ms. Pik would be choosing ten girls today. She was a shoo-in.

Suddenly, the door to Ms. Pik's office opened and she stepped out. "Okay, girls, we're going to handle this as quickly as possible. I don't want to keep you on pins and needles any longer than I have to! If you'll all follow me into the next room . . . " She raised an arm and motioned them into what appeared to be a large reception room. Lining the walls were seats. "I'd like you each to stand up as I call your name. Walk around the room once, then exit through the door we just came in and take your seat outside." She paused. "Now, as you walk I want you to imagine yourselves modeling the latest fashion. I want you to think to yourself, 'I look great, I look beautiful, and I feel very comfortable in what I'm wearing.' " She smiled as everyone began to murmur. "If that's too complicated, then, how about this? Stand straight, try and relax, and look happy. Okay?"

Alexa shrugged. Actually, she was going to think her own thoughts. She was going to imagine Barry in the audience with his eyes popping out of his head. She was going to imagine her mother sitting up straight and noticing for perhaps the first time that her daughter had real star quality. And she was going to imagine her father, with tears in his eyes, pridefully admiring his daughter.

Alexa settled into a chair next to Margo.

Yes, she had her act together. This was going to be a breeze.

Time for a little trouble making.

She turned and smiled at Margo. "So, I guess

you must be pretty nervous, huh?" She reached out and patted Margo's hand. "No one's going to laugh at you. Really. You look fine."

And with that, she turned away, opened her bag, and began rummaging through the contents, looking for nothing special.

No doubt about it. She could be very rotten. Mimi would have been furious. What did she call it again? Ah, yes. Nibblin'.

She stole a sideways glance at Margo.

Good. She looked terribly shaken.

Alexa continued looking through her bag. That almost popular crowd. They were so dumb. Didn't they know by now it was dangerous messing with Alexa Craft?

She stole one more look at Margo. Whatever would Mrs. Warner do if Margo lost out today?

Alexa smiled. What a nightmare.

"She's a jerk," Michelle whispered urgently. "Don't pay any attention to her. You look great. Why would anyone laugh?"

Margo felt the tears stinging her eyes. Desperately, she tried to will them away. She felt herself losing the battle and so she shifted in her seat to face Michelle.

"I should leave," Margo whispered.

"No," Michelle insisted. "You'd never forgive yourself. And, anyway, whatever happened to the Margo who was feeling pretty for the first time?"

Margo shrugged. "Gone."

"Go get her, then," Michelle insisted quietly. "You look great. At least give it a try. Stop turning this into a test."

"Valerie Wolf," Ms. Pik called out.

A very thin girl with stick-straight blonde hair stood up and began making her way nervously around the room.

"Look at her," Michelle whispered. "She's not gorgeous, but she's trying just the same. . . . "

Margo studied her carefully. It was true. She wasn't beautiful. She wasn't even close. But she was thin. And, more importantly, no one was laughing.

"Thank you," Ms. Pik called out as Valerie walked toward the door. "Laurie O'Hara."

This time, a beautiful girl with thick blonde curly hair stood up and, with a broad smile, began walking. Margo watched her carefully. She had a nice figure, but she wasn't especially thin. She looked as if she were having a very good time. It was almost hard to notice anything else.

I can do that, Margo thought as she pulled herself up straight in her chair. She felt the panic begin to subside.

She glanced at Alexa out of the corner of her eye. She was studying Laurie O'Hara very carefully.

In fact, she looked a little worried.

"Margo Warner," Ms. Pik called out.

Margo jumped in her seat ever so slightly.

She wasn't ready. She looked at Michelle.

"Go ahead," Michelle mouthed. "You look great."

Carefully, Margo slipped the strap of her bag over her shoulder. Then she stood up and took a deep breath.

Take it slow, Margo reminded herself. This is your moment. Make it happen. She smoothed the front of her short, deep, scoop-necked burgundy jumper, wondering for the umpteenth time whether the white turtleneck she wore underneath was really the right choice.

Margo started walking. Think happy, she instructed herself. She smiled and nodded at no one in particular. She rounded the first corner.

Shoulders back. Head straight. Hold your stomach in.

She imagined her mother in the audience, beaming with pleasure. Margo's smile broadened. She imagined the whispered voices coming from the spellbound audience. "Isn't she lovely?" "Who IS that girl?" "Oh, I wish I looked like her. . . . "

Margo relaxed even more as she reached the halfway point.

This wasn't so bad.

It was the new her.

The improved her.

Margo Warner, you know, the striking one, people would say. The one who modeled at Gerrards.

Now she was approaching the door leading to the waiting area.

She had only a few more seconds to make her mark. What could she do? What would Ms. Pik notice?

A very un-Margo kind of thing. That's what.

Suddenly, she tossed back her head and laughed. Hooking her finger around the strap of her shoulder bag, she slipped it off and dangled it in back as if it were a jacket. It was a pose she'd seen in fashion magazines.

Reaching the door, she turned the knob with her free hand and walked out.

Margo took a seat near the front and heaved a sigh of relief.

It was over.

She was either beautiful or she wasn't.

It was a relief not to have to be the one to decide any longer.

Alexa walked slowly and confidently around the room. She smiled to her left. She smiled to her right. She smiled directly at Ms. Pik.

But Alexa didn't feel good at all.

Up until the moment she'd stood up, there hadn't been the faintest doubt in her mind that she'd be chosen. But, now, walking around the room, it occurred to Alexa she might not win.

What if Ms. Pik was looking for something beyond looks? Like personality? Like some sort of "actress" thing? Why else was Margo here? And half a dozen other attractive, but not gorgeous, girls?

Alexa kept walking steadily and slowly. She had to win a spot. She tossed her hair back and smiled as if to say, "What a kick this is!" Which it wasn't. On the other hand, it was the perfect showplace for her. Just the thing she needed to give her image the boost it needed.

She had to win a spot. She just did.

"Well, girls, as I expected, this was a tough job," Ms. Pik began. She smiled around the room. "You are all beautiful."

Right, Margo thought to herself, sullenly eyeing the piece of paper Ms. Pik held in her hand. We're all the most magnificent creatures you've ever seen. It's just that some of us are more magnificent than others. Suddenly, a door in the back of the room opened. Margo turned around to see Vivienne, Priscilla, and Gina enter and stand against the wall in the back.

She smiled softly and looked away. What a bunch of good pals.

"So, before I announce the girls I've chosen for the show, I would like to remind you that I'd welcome anyone who wanted to help with choosing the fashions, music, or helping with some decorating. There's a sign-up sheet by the back door, and anyone who did not get a spot, as well as any of your friends who are interested in behind-the-scenes work, please do sign on. I want this to be a teen show from soup to nuts. Anyone who helps gets a lovely new pullover from the Lillian Saunders collection."

Margo looked around the room. It didn't seem as if anyone was dying to do that. They all had their hearts set on the spotlight.

"Okay, then," Ms. Pik began. "Everyone whose name I call out, please stay. Those of you whose name I do not call, PLEASE sign up for something, and thank you!"

Margo looked down at her white woven-leather ballet slippers as Ms. Pik began announcing names.

Patti Propper, Rene Burge, Diana Finch.

Margo glanced at Michelle and smiled tentatively.

Laurie O'Hara.

Margo felt hope surge deep inside her. Laurie wasn't perfect, either . . . and yet . . .

Alexa Craft.

Margo turned to see Alexa smile and nod as if to say, "I knew all along." She cringed.

Michelle Horne, Amy Chen, Eileen Kurtis.

Margo put an arm around Michelle and hugged her. Two more names to go.

Jessica Goldman.

Margo felt a terrible pressure inside her head. She could feel the tears begin to build up inside.

"And Elizabeth Snell. Everyone else, thank you."

"Oh, Michelle." Priscilla rushed toward them. "I'm so pleased for you!"

"I think this is all pretty silly." Vivienne shook her head, reaching for Margo's hand. "Congratulations, Michelle, but honestly, all this for parading around in nice clothes in front of a slew of strangers?"

"I think it's fun!" Gina protested. "I wish I had the time to try out for something like this. . . . "

Margo gently pulled her hand away from Vivienne's and started walking toward the door.

"Sorry, Margo," Alexa called out from behind her.

Margo nodded.

"This isn't your thing, though, anyway, is it?"

"No, it isn't, thank goodness," Vivienne snapped, descending upon them. "Why don't you shut up, Alexa. You can be as mindless as this event, and that's nothing to be proud of. Believe me."

Alexa stared at her, speechless, for a long moment, and then hurried out the door. Vivienne turned and smiled at Margo, but her smile quickly melted away.

"What's wrong? Why are you staring at me like that?"

"You guys should have stopped me," Margo practically hissed.

"Stopped you from what?" Priscilla said, joining them at the door. "Excuse me," she muttered as someone pushed past her.

"Stopped me from making a fool of myself," Margo replied coolly. "Stopped me from trying to be someone I'm not."

"Now, wait a minute," Priscilla protested.

"What's going on?" Michelle whispered. "I have to get back in the room. What are you all talking about?" She slipped an arm around Margo. "Would you consider signing up for something? We've been through this together, and I'm not sure I can do it without you being around!"

"No way," Margo replied. "And remind myself every day of what I'm not? Forget it."

"Wait a minute, what aren't you?" Priscilla asked. "I'm confused. You're not a teen model? Today? At Gerrards? Neither are eighty other girls who tried out!"

Margo shook her head. "You don't understand."

"No. YOU don't," Priscilla sighed.

"I think we need to call a meeting tomorrow," Vivienne concluded firmly. "At which time we'll discuss this entire absurd situation."

"No thanks," Margo whispered.

"Not accepted," Vivienne shook her head. "That's not what The Practically Popular Crowd is about, and you know it. Be there. My house. Four o'clock." She looked around. Everyone nodded.

Margo pushed past them.

The personality kid was not in the mood to be a good sport.

"Honey, is that you?" Mrs. Warner's voice rang through the air as Margo closed the door behind her. A chair scraped across the kitchen floor, and her mother appeared in the doorway.

"Tell me. I can't read the expression on your face. . . . "

Margo gazed at her mother evenly.

What to do.

The truth would hurt her. Which wasn't all bad. After all, she deserved it. Sort of. On the other hand, she'd been hurt enough by so many things. . . .

And, of course, then there was Margo. What kind of scene could she tolerate right now?

Not much of one. That was for sure.

There really was no choice.

Margo smiled. "I'm in. I was chosen," she said calmly, half hoping her mother would see through it.

"Margo!!!" Mrs. Warner practically screeched.

"How fabulous! How marvelous!" She held Margo away from her by the shoulders and studied her face. "Sweetie, you don't look so excited."

"I'm tired," Margo shrugged. "You know I've been very nervous. I think I'll go upstairs. . . . "

"Fine, fine." Mrs. Warner nodded understandingly. "I can't wait till the show, dear. I really can't. You Kelly girl, you . . . "

Margo smiled, walked over to the cookie bin, and pulled out four vanilla sandwiches. What have you done? a voice inside her head cried out. Are you nuts?!

"Honey," Mrs. Warner began tentatively, eyeing the sweets in her daughter's hand, "do you think that's a good idea?"

Margo shrugged. "I'm celebrating," she replied evenly. Abruptly, she turned toward the stairs.

Just a few more seconds, she whispered to herself. Hold on. Slowly she mounted the steps. They seemed endless but, a minute later, finally inside her room, Margo gently closed the door. Beaten, she sank down on her bed and allowed the tears to flow.

The quiet she craved, however, proved elusive. Aurora Warner's words began to echo from every corner of her room. "Kelly girl! Kelly girl!" Margo's tears grew more intense. "I'm not a Kelly girl," she whispered into her pillow. "I'm a Margo person. Why can't that be enough?"

13

"**R**ise and shine, you Saturday morning eager beavers!"

Alexa rolled over and clicked off her alarm clock radio. Then she tucked both hands behind her head and smiled at the ceiling. The image began to form just as clearly as it had the night before.

A *Teen* magazine cover. There she was. Hair swept back over her shoulders. A lemon-yellow turtleneck setting off her soft clear complexion. Soft pink lipstick highlighting her lips, and a delicate blue on her eyelids. Dangling from her ears, a pair of . . .

"Darling, we're leaving now," her mother's voice accompanied a soft knock at the door. "Have a good time with Larry! And congratulations again! I'm writing it into my schedule at work!"

Alexa grinned. Yes. She'd finally done it. Her mother was definitely into this modeling thing. Who knew? Maybe she'd start using her in a commercial or two! Alexa shook her head slightly as the smile began to fade. Of course, it might have been nice if her mother had gotten Barry's name right.

Pushing back the covers, Alexa hopped out of bed.

This was going to be interesting.

A double date with Barry, David, and some bimbo.

Alexa began rummaging around in the bathroom closet, looking for her special golden highlighting shampoo.

Of course, maybe she wasn't a bimbo. She frowned. It was good when they were bimbos. And not too cute.

That way she could feel . . . well . . . superior.

Alexa smiled. It was easier to shine that way.

Stepping into the shower, Alexa conditioned her hair twice, quickly dried herself off, and slipped into a pair of skintight jeans and a white long-sleeved T-shirt with pink embroidered flowers at the sleeves and collar.

She was in the middle of blow-drying her hair when Mimi walked in.

"I'm takin' a walk into town, Lexa, baby. Anything you need?"

Alexa grinned. "Barry."

Mimi shook her head. "You still on him? I heard you talkin' the other night. I almost fell asleep. . . . " She started chuckling. "Oh, Lexa, you crack me up."

"What do you mean?" Alexa asked defensively.

"I thought it was a pretty good discussion." She tried to remember what they'd talked about, but nothing came to mind. Odd.

"Sure it was," Mimi nodded. "I know how much you like talkin' 'bout the problems with the high school library. And swimming."

Oh, yeah. That's what they'd talked about. Yuk. Still . . .

"No fair, Mimi," Alexa insisted. "We also talked about my tennis game. I liked that!"

"Yes," Mimi nodded again solemnly. "You told him the scores. Hmmmmm. Kept me on the edge of my seat. Let me tell you . . . "

"Mimi, why are you doing this?" Alexa muttered. She turned her head upside down and began brushing it dry. "Stop it."

"Because I hate to see you wasting your time on things that don't matter."

"Maybe not to you," Alexa snapped.

"You, either," Mimi smiled. And with that, she gave Alexa's hair a playful tug and was gone.

Alexa listened to her heavy steps on the stairs. Mimi could be an absolute pain.

Barry and she were doing just fine. So what if it didn't feel great. Things took time.

Suddenly, Alexa rushed to her bedroom door, threw it open, and called out, "Hey, Mimi. I thought you said relationships take work!"

"They do," Mimi called back. "But first you got to have one."

*　　*　　*

"You roller skate really well, Alexa," Barry smiled at her nicely. He gripped her hand tightly.

Alexa wasn't sure if he was doing it out of affection or fear of falling.

"Thanks," she replied. She stole a quick look at his perfect profile. He was absolutely the best-looking guy at Port Andrews High.

And he was her date.

Alexa tossed her hair back over her shoulders and smiled up at the sun. So there were lots of long, lingering silences between them. So she was sometimes afraid to speak. Didn't lots of people feel that way sometimes? Sure they did.

What a glorious day. Here she was . . .

The sound of hysterical laughter directly behind Alexa interrupted her thoughts. David and Joanna were zooming over.

"Hi, guys!" David called out.

Suddenly, Alexa felt an arm slip around her waist. "Hey, Barry. Let me borrow her for just a moment." And with a few fast moves, David placed Joanna's hand in Barry's and pulled Alexa out into the center of the path.

"So, how's it going?" David asked, his arm still around her waist. He was taking broad, even strokes, and Alexa found herself matching them easily. It felt lovely.

Also a little bizarre. Quickly she stole a look

over her shoulder. Barry and Joanna were way behind.

But it was a funny thing. She didn't mind all that much.

Joanna was no competition, anyway.

"I'm going with Barry to the show, you know," David commented.

"How come?" Alexa asked, her voice dripping with sarcasm. "Don't you have anything better to do? I mean, modeling is so . . . so . . . what did you say? Ah, yes. Mindless."

"Maybe, but friendship isn't," Barry nodded. "Amy Chen is an old friend of mine. I promised I'd go."

Oh," Alexa murmured, feeling oddly disappointed. Funny. For a second she'd thought he was coming just to see her.

Not that she needed him there, of course.

Because she didn't. Alexa conjured up an image of Amy. All that thick, straight, beautiful hair. And that nice smile. Alexa didn't feel very happy.

"So, do you have something going with Joanna?" Alexa asked, anxious to get her mind moving in other directions. Less attractive directions.

"Oh, no. We're just good buddies," David responded quickly. "You jealous?"

Alexa started laughing. "I can't believe you! I'm here with Barry. Why would I be jealous?!"

"Just 'cause you're with someone doesn't mean you're WITH them, if you know what I mean."

"No, I don't know what you mean," Alexa found herself snapping.

"Lighten up," David smiled at her, squeezing her hand tightly. "I don't mean to make you angry. I can be a little obnoxious. I know that. You just always seem so uptight. It's cute."

Alexa was stunned into silence.

There it was again. That weird feeling.

That "David would make someone a great boyfriend" sensation.

"Let's skate over to the side," Alexa commented, pulling David by the hand. "We should wait for Barry and Joanna."

She turned around to look for them, and moments later spotted Barry and Joanna busily talking on a bench. Seeing Alexa waiting up ahead, Barry waved and stood up.

Alexa smiled and started skating toward him.

Barry was definitely more her type than David.

David was just too . . . too . . . average looking. Except for his eyes. They were really nice and sparkly. That's why girls liked him. Not that they fell all over him. No. Not like Barry.

Yes. Barry was her equal.

Still, David deserved someone really neat.

Someone like . . .

Alexa tried really hard to think of someone. But she just couldn't.

14

"So! How's my gorgeous daughter?" chirped Mrs. Warner as she danced into the kitchen Saturday morning. She looked over Margo's shoulder to see what she was eating.

"Ah ha! A fresh fruit salad. Good! Also some dry whole wheat toast, perhaps. It'll give you energy."

"Right." Margo didn't look up.

"I know what you're thinking," Mrs. Warner chuckled. "You think I'm going to drive you crazy about this. But I'm not! So there! I don't want to spoil this for you. It's your show!" She laughed again. "Of course, I feel a little like I'm living it, too, but, well, I'm a mother!"

And with that, she grabbed a piece of fruit herself, waved, and practically tap danced out of the kitchen on her way to the office.

Margo put her spoon down, leaned back against the chair, and stared at the ceiling.

Yes. Mrs. Warner was definitely a mother.

Unfortunately for them both, she had the wrong daughter.

"Alright. Now . . . " Vivienne opened up her notebook and marked down the date. "We've called this meeting to try and help Margo deal with whatever it is that's driving her half nuts. Not," she paused to straighten her wire-rim glasses, "that I mean to sound unsympathetic."

"I didn't ask for help," Margo insisted stubbornly. "And I think it's pretty obvious what's driving me crazy." She flicked a thread off her black tunic top.

Back to fat clothes again. After all, why not?

"Not really," Priscilla began, pulling out her sketch pad and pencil. "I mean, we know you're disappointed, but . . . "

"But you figure, you wouldn't be so upset, so why should I. Right?"

"Okay. Okay. I agree," Michelle interjected. "It doesn't matter what we think we'd feel like." She paused. "So why don't you explain exactly how you feel, and we'll try to understand."

Margo sighed. How exactly did she feel?

Like a speck on the wall?

No. Some people noticed specks on walls.

"I feel like a big nothing. Even worse. A moron."

"Because you didn't win a modeling spot?" Vivienne yelped.

"No." Margo sighed. "Because I actually thought I would win a spot. That's why."

Michelle nodded. "Okay. I see."

"But there's more," Margo went on. She looked around the room slowly. It was hard to tell if they'd be patient with this part.

"I know you guys think I'm great. Fun to be with. A leader. All that stuff. But I'm tired of being the one who weighs too much. I'm tired of always feeling like OTHER girls are the real pretty ones, but I have to settle for bubbly or cute."

"I think you're pretty," Gina insisted. "I've told you that lots of time. You are, you know."

"Tell that to Ms. Pik," Margo grumbled. "Besides. You always think everything is so simple."

"That's not true," Gina protested.

Margo looked away. Gina was right to stick up for herself. The truth was, Gina just held a lot of stuff in. She always wanted everything to be smooth.

"You know, there were lots of real pretty girls that weren't selected, either," Michelle noted.

"Easy for you to say," Margo snapped.

"Well, I'm glad that's over with!" Vivienne announced cheerfully. "I'm sure we were all wondering when Margo would get around to torturing Michelle." She looked around the room. "Does everyone feel better now?"

For a moment, there was nothing but silence. Suddenly, Gina giggled.

"I do."

"It felt good," Margo nodded. She whirled around to face Michelle. "Who do you think you are anyway, Michelle? Christie Brinkley?" Then she laughed and squeezed Michelle's hand. "I deserved that spot. Not you." She looked around the room. "Can I keep going? This feels good."

"I think that's enough," Vivienne giggled. "We get the point." She paused. "But, you know, Margo, you haven't mentioned one really important thing."

"What's that?" Margo asked, suddenly feeling sick to her stomach.

"How did your mother take it?"

"My mother . . . " Margo responded dully. "Well, my mother took it fine." She smiled and looked up at the ceiling.

They would not believe what she'd done.

It was too horrifying.

"Well, that's a pleasant surprise," Priscilla remarked. "I mean, I didn't think she'd be impossible or anything, but . . . "

"No. She wasn't impossible," Margo interrupted. She had to tell them. They'd never understand what came over her, of course. But then, who would?

"Well, let's hear it for Mrs. Warner," Vivienne exclaimed.

"Actually," Margo raised both hands and stared

into Michelle's eyes. "Not so fast." She paused. "I didn't exactly tell her."

Michelle hesitated. "You mean she thinks nothing's been decided yet?" She ran a hand through her hair thoughtfully. "Well, that was probably a good idea. It gives us time to help you figure out what to say. . . . "

"Well, no, that's not quite what I mean," Margo continued, her voice now beginning to shake.

The room was completely silent now.

"I told her I won a spot."

"You're kidding," Vivienne blurted out, allowing the pen to drop from her hand. "Tell us you're kidding."

Margo felt the tears beginning to form. "I had to. I couldn't take seeing her look so disappointed. I felt bad enough as it was. I didn't want to let her down. . . . " Suddenly, she made a fist and pounded on the floor. "Of course, if it wasn't for her and her stupid Kelly girl garbage, I wouldn't have even tried out." She looked around the room accusingly. "And you guys didn't help much, either."

"Now, wait a minute," Vivienne snapped. "You just got through telling us it was YOU who wanted to be beautiful. You did this modeling thing to prove something to you, not . . . "

"Okay, Vivienne," Priscilla interrupted soothingly. "Margo is just upset. She obviously did it for many reasons."

"Yeah, I'm upset," Margo cried out. "But I wouldn't be in this position if everyone hadn't encouraged me. I'm such an idiot for believing all of you!"

"First of all," Michelle proclaimed loudly, "let us not forget you made callbacks. That's more than half the girls who tried out can say. Okay? Let's not forget that."

Margo fell silent. That was true. She'd forgotten about that. Still, what did that matter in the end? For all she knew, it was a big mistake. Ms. Pik might have meant to call someone else's name.

"Second," Michelle went on, "blaming everyone else because you feel bad isn't going to help. And third," Michelle added, folding her arms across her chest, "are you going to tell me that just because you weren't chosen to model clothes, it then follows you aren't pretty?"

"Well, what else am I supposed to think?" Margo muttered. "That I was too pretty? That Ms. Pik was afraid everyone would stare at me instead of the clothes?" She started to giggle at the thought. "Yes. That must have been it."

Michelle smiled at her friend warmly. "No. But let's look at a worst case. Let's say she didn't select you because, as you've pointed out hundreds of times to all of us, you aren't tall, long legged, and really thin. Let's say that's true. So how come that means you aren't still pretty?"

Margo shrugged. It sounded crazy, but somehow it just did.

Gina shook her head. "You're very stubborn."

"You're also in trouble," Vivienne noted. "Let's get back to your mother."

"You're going to have to tell her the truth, and the sooner the better," Priscilla offered sympathetically. "You can't let her go on thinking you're in. She'll tell her friends. She'll make plans to come and see you. . . . "

"I know," Margo sighed, lowering her head. "But how? When?"

"Short and sweet is best," Vivienne suggested. "Mom, I have something to tell you. The truth is they didn't pick me to model. I didn't tell you the truth because I was too upset myself and I didn't want to see you feeling bad, too." Vivienne threw both hands in the air. "Voila!"

"Maybe you could tell her," Margo murmured hopefully. "That was good."

"No way," Vivienne laughed. "This is your nightmare."

"You're not kidding," Margo sighed. "This whole thing has been nothing but a . . . "

"Well, you know," Priscilla said thoughtfully as she began shading in the bookcase she was drawing, "it doesn't have to be . . . "

"What do you mean?" Margo looked at her with surprise. "I want to be beautiful. I find out I'm not. I think I can model. I find out I can't. I dream I'm finally going be something like the daughter my mother always wanted, only I discover it's out of the question." She paused as her voice began to shake. "I would have been happy just for that one moment when I could shine. For me. For my mother." She looked down at her hands. "That sounds like a nightmare to me."

Priscilla smiled. "Well, first of all, I'm not sure you've got all your facts straight. I mean, they are a little colored by your emotions right now. But let's put that aside." She paused. "Sometimes, if you just think creatively, you can find other ways to make a dream happen."

"Like what?" Margo practically snapped.

"I don't know yet," Priscilla answered matter-of-factly. "But let's not forget we're The Practically Popular Crowd. We're a team. We might just be able to come up with a way for you to have 'your moment.' "

"Terrific. Well, I feel better," Margo snarled. "Good luck."

"Boy, you get mean when you're hurt," Vivienne piped up. "Priscilla's just trying to help."

Margo stared down at the floor. These were her closest friends in the world. Why was she taking everything out on them?

"I'm sorry," she said softly. "This is not your fault. It's not even totally my mother's. I wanted this so much . . . "

"That's okay," Michelle smiled. "Just tell your mother the truth. Put that behind you and then maybe we'll be able to think of something." She giggled. "I have to admit, though, I don't know what!"

"Me, neither," Margo moaned.

"You never know what can come of things," Priscilla intoned. "A person just has to be open. . . . "

"I hate it when you get poetic," Viv laughed.

"Do you want me to come with you when you tell your mother?" Michelle asked helpfully. "I will."

"No." Margo shook her head.

That would not be necessary.

There was one thing her friends didn't quite understand.

Mostly because she didn't want to tell them.

There was no way she could tell her mother the truth.

No way at all.

15

Margo sat, trembling, in the back of the classroom. So far so good. Not a word had been said. Somehow she'd been sure the whole school would have heard of her humiliation.

But it hadn't. The entire wretched experience still belonged completely to her. Margo heaved a heavy sigh.

Oh, joy.

"So, without further ado, I'd like to call Margo Warner to the front of the class." Lisa Meade began stepping to the side. "She had a long meeting with the head of the Port Andrews Committee for the Homeless and apparently she has quite a few things to say."

"When doesn't she?" a voice called out from the back of the room. Margo tensed as she started forward. It was just an ordinary tease, but it felt like a smack in the face.

"At least she's got something to say, which is more than we can say about you," another voice retorted.

Margo smiled softly. Lighten up, a voice inside her head entreated. This is no longer a beauty contest. It's over. Hardly anyone knows about what happened with you at Gerrards. Margo looked around the room. It was amazing how something that was so important to her meant so little to everyone else.

"First of all," Margo began slowly and deliberately. Pace yourself, she thought. People listen if you give them time to listen. "Mr. Fox is thrilled we are donating the proceeds from our bake sale to the homeless cause. And also about the ways we could help the children. He reports that what we read in the papers does almost no justice to the desperation of the situation."

Her eyes traveled around the room. Alexa was studying herself in a mirror. Julie was running a comb through her hair. Bill was leaning back in his chair as if he were about to go to sleep. Her eyes rested on Vivienne, who was listening intently. Margo smiled straight at her appreciatively, and then looked quickly around the room once more. What a scene.

This had never happened before.

Everyone looked so bored.

So concerned about other things.

So uninspired by what she was saying.

"He also was very interested in seeing whether we could help in other ways to bring money into the committee. He thought perhaps we could talk to the storekeepers that we frequent the most. Maybe we could place boxes for donations there, or start a raffle and sell them. . . . "

Once again, Margo's eyes traveled about the room.

James was flipping through a sports magazine.

Margo spotted Paul doodling on a blank pad.

She sighed. Of course, a really good-looking girl would have everyone's attention in a minute. In two seconds they'd be hanging on her very word. Just as they used to when she . . .

Suddenly Margo looked up at the ceiling and began chewing thoughtfully on the inside of her lip.

This was ridiculous. Her meetings were always lively. Sometimes even funny. But this . . . Margo ran a hand through her thick mop of curls. This was like a meeting of dead people.

Margo took a deep breath and placed both hands on the desk before her. Okay, so she wasn't beautiful. But one thing she wasn't, one thing no one could ever say about her, was that she was a bore.

"I have an idea," she announced, nodding at no one in particular. "Let's just discuss for one second, please, what each of you would do if the bell rang, and you had no real place to call home. Other than, say, a motel room?" She looked around the room. "Just for the sake of argument. What would you do?"

"I'd go to the pizza place," a voice called out with a giggle.

Margo shook her head. "No good. You don't have money."

"I'd go to a friend's house."

Again, Margo shook her head. "Your friend's mother is tired of having you. . . . "

"I'd go to Gerrards," Alexa called out. "How about you?"

For a moment, Margo froze. She could hear a few voices whispering urgently, but for the most part a chorus of "Whats?" filled the air.

"Again, no money," Margo responded, more timidly than she'd have liked. Darn Alexa. She could shake up Mount Everest.

"Not what I mean!" Alexa sang out challengingly.

"Oh, forgive us," Vivienne called out sarcastically. "We forgot. Let's all give Alexa a round of applause for achieving the high honor of being a walking clothes mannequin at a fashion show." She began clapping, as others laughingly joined in.

Margo stared down at the floor, willing the tears away. In one second, everyone would know. She could feel it in her bones.

"Well, I'd try to avoid going to the motel," Gina suddenly called out loudly. "Maybe to a library . . . "

Margo shot her a grateful look as the class immediately began quieting down. She nodded and, taking a deep breath, looked around the room. They were all staring at her expectantly now. The way they used to.

As if she were really somebody.

As if she were . . .Ms. Homeless of Port Andrews Junior High.

Margo almost laughed out loud at the image.

There she stood, a bouquet of red roses clutched in one hand, sporting a golden crown styled with a nail and hammer motif, passing out house keys to every homeless person on earth.

Margo frowned.

It was certainly no match for Miss Georgia Peach.

But then, what could she ever do that would be?

Alexa threw her books onto the antique hallway table and gazed at herself in the floor-to-ceiling mirrors.

"I'm telling you, Robin. I could just tell. Ms. Pik thought I was a natural. I practically floated around the room during rehearsals." She twisted around to look at the back of her dress. She frowned. "I'm so wrinkled. I hope that didn't interfere with . . . "

"Alexa! I'm sure you were great!" Robin laughed. "This isn't Paris! No one's expecting a professional! I mean . . . "

"You may not see the importance of this event, Robin," Alexa replied stiffly, "but this is a very big deal to me. This IS Paris to me. I've got my parents coming. I've got Barry coming. And if I don't look one hundred percent, I'm going to blow my very first opportunity to really show what I've got."

Alexa turned back to her reflection in the mirror.

Now there was an interesting point. What exactly did she have? Alexa frowned. Actually, it was easier to take it from another angle. What did she want to have?

Star quality.

Yes. That would be nice. It was also realistic. She did have something that seemed to make people sit up and take notice.

And what else?

Depth would be nice. Substance. Meaningfulness. That kind of thing. Like Michelle Horne. What was it about her that always seemed so . . . important?

Alexa cocked her head to one side. She had some of that. Probably not enough, though.

"Robin," Alexa began slowly, "do you think I have . . . well . . . depth?"

Robin hesitated. "You know, I never thought about that before."

"Well, think about it now," Alexa urged her, trying not to let her annoyance show through. "I mean, Ms. Pik says it's important to let more than just your beauty out. You have to let something from inside show as well."

Alexa envisioned Michelle walking about the room. She had looked so warm, so real. So interesting. Alexa grimaced. Of course, they weren't talking at all. Not after the job she'd done on Margo.

Robin nodded. "Oh, well, sure. I see your confidence in the way you walk, Alexa. And I see your mind working in your eyes, sometimes. Sure. You have depth."

Alexa nodded.

Robin was full of it.

Suddenly, she missed Mona terribly.

Mona had depth enough for both of them.

16

Margo stood outside Gerrards Wednesday afternoon and checked her watch.

Michelle would be out in a few minutes. Of course, she could go in and watch the rehearsals.

Look at all the pretty clothes.

Not to mention girls.

Margo shook her head. No way. Ms. Personality would just keep standing outside. Thank you very much.

Tomorrow was time enough. She would be there to watch Michelle. That was plenty.

"Hi," Priscilla said cheerfully as she arrived at Margo's side carrying a large pop poster she'd painted for the show. "Going in?"

"Are you kidding?" Margo chuckled. "That's all I need." She turned and studied Priscilla accusingly. "By the way. I'm still waiting. Where is my moment? From where I sit, there's only one thing left yet to happen that hasn't. And that's Aurora Warner learning the truth."

"You've got to tell her tonight," Priscilla said

somberly. "You have to. You can't let her show up and see that you're not in the show. I mean, of course, something could happen and you could end up . . . "

"Why do you keep saying things like that?" Margo snapped. "What's going to happen? Besides, I don't need to be a runner up."

"I know," Priscilla sighed miserably. "I guess I was just hoping for something to make Ms. Pik feel she needed a few more people. But so far, it hasn't happened. I mean, there were so many pretty clothes to choose from, including this great line of denim wear, but Ms. Pik only wanted to include one piece from the bunch because there were only twenty girls and . . . " her voice trailed off. Priscilla shrugged.

Margo felt like kissing her.

"Oh, Priscilla, even The Practically Popular Crowd can't fix everything. I guess I'm just not supposed to feel really beautiful. I'm supposed to feel, well, other things. It's not as glamorous but, hey . . . "

"Once you tell your mother, you'll feel better," Priscilla urged her. "Frankly, I think that's your biggest problem."

"Well, actually, my other problem," Margo commented, anxious to get away from what to do about her mother, "is helping Bob Fox get this community to wise up his organization. I still haven't gotten more than one or two stores to put donation boxes on their counters, not that I've been trying that hard, and . . . "

Suddenly, Margo stopped talking. She looked up at Gerrards and back at Priscilla.

Following Margo's gaze, Priscilla shrugged. "It's worth a try."

"Do you think?" Margo went on thoughtfully.

"Sure. They have lots of counters. Why not?" Priscilla suggested.

Margo nodded solemnly. Of all places. She'd probably make a mint here.

"The way I see it, Gerrards owes you one," Priscilla said, grinning broadly. She held up her poster for them both to consider. "You better believe it."

Margo studied the poster.

"Wait a minute," she suddenly cried out. "Forget the boxes." She pointed to the sign Priscilla was holding. "The show! A benefit! It's perfect!"

For a long moment, Priscilla was quiet. Then she grabbed Margo's arm with a triumphant look on her face. "That's it!" she whispered.

"I wonder if it's a problem Gerrards isn't in Port Andrews?" Margo went on.

"Doesn't matter," Priscilla insisted. "It can't matter. A lot of the models are from Port Andrews." She excitedly began reciting their names.

"Of course." Margo turned her head sharply away as if she'd been slapped. The models. That again. For a second she'd almost forgotten. Suddenly, she was sorry the idea of working with Gerrards had occurred to her at all. It was the last place she wanted to be. "It's a little late, but I'll talk to Ms. Pik about a benefit." She paused, staring at her friend curiously. "But frankly, Priscilla, I can't understand why you look so excited. I mean, this homeless thing hasn't exactly been your number one interest in life."

"Never mind," Priscilla waved the comment away. "Quick. Let's come up with a plan to turn this into a benefit."

"Well," Margo replied, "let's see. Maybe Gerrards could donate a small percentage of sales to the committee." She paused. "You and I could design a flyer to be given out at the show. Then, when anyone who has one buys something at Gerrards, they hand it in, and a dollar gets put aside from their purchase to be given to our fund. Something like that."

Priscilla grinned. "Very clever."

Margo shrugged. "Big deal."

"Well, let's go." Priscilla began dragging her toward the door. "This is what I meant. This is something good. You see? I was right! You need to discuss this with Ms. Pik right now. There's no time to lose."

For an instant, Margo pulled back. "Priscilla, you do it." She could feel the distress creeping over her like a dark, unfriendly blanket. "Here I am again. Good ole Margo Warner. Never the beauty. Always the brains, or the leader, or . . . "

Priscilla clung to Margo's hand. "Don't be so sure," she murmured.

"What do you mean?" Margo asked, allowing herself to be led through the front doors of Gerrards Department Store.

"Trust me," Priscilla replied. "This is step number one."

"To what?" Margo cried out impatiently.

But Priscilla simply wouldn't answer.

There was just too much to do.

17

"I'm so excited you're going to be there . . . " Alexa practically purred into the phone. "I know it's not your kind of thing."

That's right. Alexa smiled to herself. Let him know you understand the sort of guy he is.

"Well, that's true," Barry replied. "But you're excited. That's important."

For a moment, Alexa was stunned. Barry had never said anything like that before. Well, he'd be saying that and much, much more after he got an eyeful of her tomorrow.

A vision of Mona flashed across her mind. This was as good a time as any to check out the status of that relationship.

"So tell me, have you been helping Mona anymore on her debate thing?" Alexa asked, as if she were merely curious.

"Nope. She said she was doing fine."

Alexa nodded. Obviously, Mona had decided she'd better steer clear of Barry. That was good of her.

So why weren't they talking? Alexa sighed. Because, as usual, Alexa had stirred up a brush fire and forgotten to put it out.

"Well, actually, Barry," Alexa purred once more, "I think it's time for me to get off. I haven't had dinner yet, and then after that I need my rest tonight. . . . "

"Oh, yeah, sure," Barry replied almost too quickly. "You do that. I'll see you tomorrow afternoon at Gerrards. Okay?"

"Yes," Alexa smiled. "Bye-bye." And with that, she hung up the phone, slipped on the pair of high-heeled shoes she would wear tomorrow, and stood up. She wobbled ever so slightly.

Good thing she'd brought them home to practice.

Alexa walked to the top of the staircase.

"Mimi!" she called out. "Could you come here one second?"

"Sure, Lexa baby," Mimi replied, appearing a moment later in the foyer. "What's cookin'? I was just tryin' to fix that shelf in the den that keeps fallin'."

"Well, could you watch me coming down these stairs? I figure if I can handle steps gracefully in these shoes without staring at the floor, I can certainly do it walking down a flat runway."

"Okay. I'm watchin'," Mimi smiled. "But, Lexa baby, hold onto that bannister. I'd hate to see you flyin' head first . . . "

129

"Oh, shush." Alexa waved away Mimi's worries with one hand, and flashed a big smile. "Everything's a near disaster with you. I can't imagine how you get up in the morning."

Holding her head high, with her eyes focused on the small pane of glass embedded in the top of the front door, Alexa began her descent.

"And here is Ms. Alexa Craft," Alexa began, trying to imitate Ms. Pik's voice, "in a delightful, and slightly daring, prom dress created from a shade of blue satin guaranteed to show off any complexion."

Alexa looked from the right to the left. She nodded. She smiled. Her hand rested ever so lightly on the bannister.

After all, she'd be leaning on absolutely nothing tomorrow.

"Notice the sweetheart neckline and touch of lace."

Alexa continued slowly down the sweeping staircase. She could see her parents now. Sitting together, all smiles, gazing lovingly at her. And there, a few chairs over, would be Barry. And David.

Alexa smiled now. At them both. She could just see David now. Twinkling at her. Yes, he was definitely a kick.

"The moonlit glow of this infatuating number guarantees an evening of . . . "

Suddenly, a loud crash echoed through the house.

Startled, Alexa reach for the bannister. She could feel the loss of balance as her hand grasped it just in time.

"Boy, for a minute I thought I was in real trouble. . . . " Alexa began as she watched Mimi turn toward the den. "I thought for sure I was . . . "

And then it happened.

Alexa realized what she'd done the moment she took her next step.

She'd forgotten about the shoes.

Once again, she caught herself by grabbing the bannister, but not before she felt her ankle twist and bend painfully as she crumpled, gracefully but miserably, onto the carpeted steps.

"Darling, I didn't expect to see you!" Mrs. Warner sang out happily, as she waltzed into the kitchen Thursday afternoon. "No final rehearsals?! You must be so excited."

Margo placed the glass of water she was sipping on the counter. This was impossible. How had she let it get this far?

"You know Lily Bardavid from the office? She's coming to see you, too. She's always been such a fan of yours, you know. She thinks you are positively lovely."

Margo nodded. "That's nice."

It was crazy.

She had to say something. What did she think was going to happen? Her mother wouldn't notice Margo wasn't in the show?

"Mom," Margo began, walking over to the kitchen window, "I have something I have to tell you." She reached for her glass. She had to hang on to something.

"Well, I'm here, dear. Is it your nerves? You know, before the beauty pageant I was in, I almost backed out. Can you believe that?"

Margo looked away. No. She couldn't.

She studied her mother's face. She looked so excited. So pleased. So proud.

She was positively glowing.

Margo positively hated her.

"Mom, I didn't . . . "

Suddenly, the phone rang.

"Hello?" Mrs. Warner's cheery voice filled the green-and-white kitchen.

"Oh, yes! Hello, Mr. Craft. Certainly, I'd love to show your clients that house again. Of course." She paused. "No. Unfortunately I cannot meet you tomorrow afternoon. You see, my daughter is in the fashion show, too, and afterwards we're going to celebrate." Smiling brightly, Mrs. Warner turned and winked at Margo. "But I'm going into the office for an hour or two now. Let me call you from there to set something up." Again she paused. "Good. And thanks. Yes. I am very proud."

Mrs. Warner hung up the phone and turned back to Margo.

"So. Dear. You were saying. . . . "

Margo stood staring at her quietly for a long moment.

The whole thing was just too much.

And it was all her mother's fault.

She couldn't let go. She couldn't be her and let Margo be Margo. She had to push . . . push . . . push . . .

Margo could feel the anger stirring wildly inside her. She didn't deserve to know. If she couldn't see who Margo really was, then it was time for her to at least see who Margo really wasn't.

Yes. The time had come.

So what if she'd be embarrassed.

Who cared?

Embarrassment had become Margo's middle name.

Embarrassment Kelly, to be exact.

Early Thursday evening, Alexa lay stunned in the Crafts' deep-red, plush, paisleyed family den. Her eyes traveled about the room. It looked like a funeral parlor. Her leg, heavily bandaged, was elevated on four pillows.

Her crutches lay on the floor beside the sofa.

"What am I going to do?" Alexa sobbed, staring through tears at her father. "It was going to be my moment. I was going to look so beautiful. . . . "

"These things happen," Mr. Craft sighed. "You just have to pick up the pieces and go on."

Alexa nodded. Why was it he never said what she needed to hear? Even a "You always look beautiful to me," would have helped.

Actually a lot.

Alexa studied her father for a long moment. He was, for an older person, really very handsome. She was so proud of him.

And tomorrow was supposed to have been the day he would finally feel the same way about her. . . .

Alexa felt the tears beginning to flow once more. "Thanks for changing your appointment around to see me. You can get going now."

"Thanks?" Mr. Craft said, cupping her chin in his hand. "You're my daughter." Kissing Alexa lightly on the cheek, he stood up and walked out of the room.

"And you love me . . . right?" Alexa whispered, after he closed the door halfway behind him. She sighed. He just wasn't good at saying nice stuff.

Alexa reached for a tissue and shrugged. Actually, she wasn't good at believing nice stuff, even if someone said it plain as day. So what did it matter?

Alexa turned toward the phone. She needed to talk to someone. Anyone. She paused.

Well, that wasn't exactly true.

She needed to talk to Mona.

Alexa reached for the phone and hesitated. If the tables were turned, she'd have wanted to hang up on Mona. She frowned.

On the other hand, Mona didn't get like that.

She didn't hang on to being angry.

She didn't carry grudges.

Alexa sighed. Actually, sometimes she couldn't figure out why Mona put up with her garbage. A soft smile began to play across her lips. The truth was, of course, that Mona didn't put up with it.

After all, she hadn't called for a solid week.

Alexa dialed her number and a moment later, she heard Mona's warm voice saying hello.

"It's me," Alexa began, suddenly feeling her chest begin to heave. "Mona . . . "

"What's the matter!" Mona cried out with alarm in her voice. "Tell me!"

"I . . . I . . . twisted my ankle," Alexa blurted out. "And now it's all over! I can't model tomorrow."

"Oh, Alexa! How awful!" Mona sighed. "And you wanted to do this so badly. What can I do to cheer you up?"

Alexa fell back against her pillow with relief.

Mona understood. They weren't so far apart after all.

"Mona, I'm sorry I've been so irritable lately," she murmured. "I just haven't felt good about Barry. And I missed spending time with you and . . ."

"Forget it, Alexa," Mona laughed. "I'm used to you. I didn't think we weren't friends anymore. I just figured we were taking a vacation."

"Could you please come over and keep me company tomorrow?" Alexa asked meekly. "You know, while the show is going on?"

"Sure," Mona replied quickly. "I will."

A soft knock on the open door interrupted the conversation.

Alexa looked up.

"How you doin', honey?" Mimi asked, walking into the den.

"Oh, just great," Alexa sighed. She motioned for Mimi to stay. "Mona, I'll call you later, okay?"

Alexa hung up and turned to Mimi. "Well, isn't this terrific."

"Hmmmm," Mimi nodded. "But you know, I've been thinkin'. Maybe you could do this modelin' thing anyway."

"You've got to be kidding." Alexa practically sputtered. "I'd make a complete fool of myself."

"No, you wouldn't, honey," Mimi shook her

head vigorously. "You're too darn pretty. But you might look real brave and excitin'."

Alexa shook her head. "No way. I'd look ridiculous. Desperate. Besides, Ms. Pik would never go for it."

"I swear, Lexa, you talkin' like you sprained your brain, not your ankle. What happened to your fightin' spirit?"

"I'm supposed to look romantic and graceful. I'm wearing a prom dress," Alexa snapped.

Mimi shrugged. "Romance is not in the ankles. So wear somethin' else."

Alexa shook her head. "You don't understand. It's not that simple."

Mimi stood up. "I'm not sayin' it's easy. I'm not sayin' it would even work. I'm just sayin' if anyone could turn this around, it's you, baby. And I'll tell you something else . . . "

"What?" Alexa asked irritably, not at all sure she wanted to know.

"If you do get yourself up there on that runway, no one is ever goin' to forget it." She smiled at Alexa. "Think about that."

"Yeah, they'll never forget what a jerk I was," Alexa replied.

"Crutches don't make jerks." Mimi shook her head. "People do."

"I can't do it," Alexa insisted, just as the phone began to ring.

"Alexa?" An unfamiliar voice rang across the wire.

"Yes?"

"It's Margo's mom. Aurora Warner. How are you, dear?"

Alexa hesitated. She didn't feel like going into it. "Oh, fine," she murmured softly.

"Oh, you must be so excited," Mrs. Warner exclaimed. "I know Margo is! She cannot wait to get up there tomorrow!"

Alexa just stared at the phone. "Excuse me?"

"Oh, yes. Just think. The two of you! Modeling!"

Alexa smiled for the first time in hours. This was too good to be true.

Here it was. Her chance.

And it couldn't have come at a better time. She was just so darn angry.

Revenge would feel, well, comforting.

Alexa looked at Mimi, who was watching her curiously.

"Could you hold on a minute, please?" Alexa asked politely into the phone.

"Yes, dear, but I just wanted to speak to your father. . . . "

"Of course," Alexa responded quickly. "Just a sec."

She turned to Mimi. "Could I be alone, please?"

Mimi nodded. "Sure, hon. You just think about what I said."

Alexa nodded. "I will."

Mimi walked out.

Alexa took a deep breath and turned back to the phone. "Mrs. Warner?"

"Yes, dear?"

Alexa hesitated. This was as stinky as she ever got. In fact, it was almost too miserable for her. That club of theirs would be furious.

"Alexa?"

"Yes. Mrs. Warner." Alexa leaned back on her pillow. "I think you should know something." Alexa's finger traced the pattern of a heavily brocaded paisley pillow lying beside her.

What could they do to her, anyway?

Nothing. That's what.

"Mrs. Warner," she began, forcing sadness into her voice. Regret. Almost misery. "I don't know how to tell you this . . . but . . . Margo is not in the show."

A heavy silence followed.

"Hello?" Alexa said softly. Knowingly.

"What do you mean?" Mrs. Warner replied hoarsely.

Alexa smiled. "Let me explain," she murmured, with heartbreaking empathy in every breath. Acting was fun.

She began talking.

But one minute later, mid-conversation, somewhere between the "poor Margo's" and "such lovely clothes," Alexa suddenly froze.

There actually was a way to be in the show.
A very workable way, in fact.
Alexa fought back the tears.
The only problem was, exposing Margo might have just blown it.

18

Margo tacked the flyer up on her bulletin board, stepped back, and nodded. It did the job.

In fact, it looked fantastic. Margo smiled sadly. Well, at least Ms. Pik had done something right. She'd seen the merits of turning the fashion show into a benefit almost immediately. One call to her boss and it was done.

As Vivienne liked to say, "Voila!"

Margo frowned. So why did it feel like a booby prize? And why did Priscilla keep acting as if she was up to something? What could she possibly . . .

Margo heard the front door slam loudly. Lewis. Good thing her mother wasn't home. He'd have really caught it for that. Southern ladies didn't go for loud noises.

Margo threw herself down on the bed and desperately tried to shut out her next thought. It didn't work.

Could she really go through with it? Could she

really let her mother show up expecting to see Margo strutting her stuff?

Margo felt her head begin to pound. What else could she do? Say something now? Now, after all this time? Watch her mother crumble with disappointment?

No. She couldn't face it. She'd crumble, too. So far, she'd managed. So she wasn't gorgeous. So she'd never model. Not even for a day. Margo looked up at her flyer. She could pull things like that off. Maybe it wasn't as exciting, or romantic, or glorious. But it was something. . . .

Margo could feel the anger stirring again. Her mother had to leave her alone. And, starting tomorrow, that's just what she was going to do. What she needed was a shock. Margo felt the tears begin to fall.

She reached for a tissue, just about the same time that her bedroom door flew wide open.

"Why?" Mrs. Warner said quietly as she stood trembling in the doorway.

For a fleeting moment, Margo wasn't sure. Maybe she knew, maybe she didn't. She stared blankly at her mother.

"I'm asking you a question. Why did you lie?"

So. Here it was. The moment she'd been dreading for an entire week. Margo stared down at the floor.

"Don't look away from me, young lady," Mrs. Warner snapped. Angrily, she walked into the bedroom and stood towering over Margo, who was sitting quietly on her bed. "I want an explanation right now. I want to know what's been going on. I want to know where you've been going all this time I thought you were at rehearsals. And most of all, I want to know how you could make up such a horrible lie."

Margo stared through her tears at the blank wall in front of her. She wanted to answer. But she had a dreadful feeling that once she started, she'd never stop. She and her mother would be old and gray and still fighting. Still crying. Still wishing they could make each other into other people.

She started to giggle. The vision of the two of them with gray hair was really rather funny. Her giggling got louder. Margo stood up.

She'd never felt so bizarre in her life. She absolutely could not stop laughing.

"Margo Warner, stop that right now," Mrs. Warner practically screamed, grabbing Margo's arm and shaking her. "Stop it, before I slap you!"

"I . . . I . . . can't," Margo sputtered. "I just think it's so . . . "

And then, suddenly, something changed. It was almost as though someone had flipped a switch.

Margo felt her chest beginning to heave. And a moment later, the laughter changed into a terrible, uncontrollable sobbing.

"No, I will not be swayed by hysteria," Mrs.

Warner insisted. "I love you, but you've been tricking me. Tears will not change the way I feel."

"Nothing ever does!" Margo cried out, now with tears streaming down her cheeks. "And you don't love me. You just love what you want me to be!"

"What are you talking about?" Mrs. Warner whispered with disbelief. "You think I don't love you?"

Margo began to tremble. "All you care about is making me into a Kelly girl. Me being just like you were. But I'm not! I'm me!"

"But Margo. Is that what this is about? You feeling unattractive? Margo Warner. Did you even try to be in this show, or was that part of this terrible thing, too? Did you try?"

"MOM," Margo shouted as loud as she could. "Get this through your head! I did try. I wanted to be a model. I did. But in the end, I didn't make it! I'm not like you. I'm not a beauty queen!"

"Honey," Mrs. Warner sighed, "you have to stop putting yourself down."

Filled with frustration, Margo grabbed her mother's hands. "Mom, that's just it. Why does not being a beauty contestant mean I'm putting myself down? Is it THAT important?" Margo looked at her mother beseechingly. "Don't you see? I don't want it to be. Maybe because I can't be that person. I don't know. But, Mom, why does it have to be the goal of every Warner, excuse me, Kelly girl, to be in a beauty pageant?"

"Well," Mrs. Warner replied quietly, "I always felt being Miss Georgia Peach was an honor. I had no idea you thought so little of it. Is that why you lied to me? To prove a point?"

"Darn it, Mom," Margo cried out. "No! I lied because I felt terrible! I wanted to win, too. I wanted to win for both of us! I knew you were desperate for me to get a spot, and I just couldn't tell you . . . and then before I knew it, it was just too late, and . . . " Margo looked up at her mother angrily.

Here it was. The real bottom line of it all.

"I've been FURIOUS at you. Furious, because I'm sick of feeling terrible that I can't be who you want. I'm even tired of feeling bad that I'm not being who I want! I want to like me. But I can't. Not with you snapping at me all the time. Where are your friends, Margo? You'd be so pretty if you lost a little weight, Margo. . . . This whole thing is your fault, too. Can't you see that?!"

Mrs. Warner leaned against the wall and studied her daughter in silence. Finally, she, too, sighed. "Margo, I'm in shock. You'll have to forgive me. I thought you really wanted to be in this show."

Margo put her head in her hands. "I did. Don't you see? I did. I'm so confused. I'm sorry. But I'm not a model. And I want to think that's okay. I do. But you won't let me. I'm very disappointed." Margo could feel the sobs coming on again. "I wanted that moment. I wanted to feel beautiful. . . . "

Mrs. Warner placed a hand tentatively on her daughter's shoulder. "Still, you should not have lied to me."

Margo shook her head.

It had been her only choice.

"It was embarrassing finding out from Alexa the way I did, calling about her father's client who needs a rental. Why, I must be a laughing stock of the whole town. . . . "

"You and me both," Margo sighed. "And I still have to go to the show tomorrow to make a little speech."

"A speech?"

"Yes, I talked them into turning the whole event into a benefit for the homeless," Margo shrugged. "No big deal."

Mrs. Warner nodded.

Margo looked away. Now, why had she expected an argument?

How ridiculous.

"Mom, I'm real tired," Margo murmured. "If you want to punish me somehow, go ahead. I just can't do this anymore."

"I have one question," Mrs. Warner said softly. "Were you so angry at me that you were just going to let me show up at Gerrards?"

Margo hesitated. And then she slowly began to

nod. "I know it was crazy. But I didn't just feel anger," she whispered. "I was ashamed, too."

"Well, I would think so. . . . " Mrs. Warner laughed sadly. "What a terrible thing to do to me."

Margo shook her head. "No, Mom. Ashamed that I wasn't up there modeling."

Mrs. Warner stood there silently for another few seconds, and then walked out, closing the door softly behind her.

Margo lay back on her bed and closed her eyes.

So it was over.

Thank goodness.

Alexa Craft.

She didn't know whether to kick her or kiss her.

19

"**I** cannot imagine what you are up to," Mona sighed, watching Alexa run a comb through her hair.

Alexa looked away. She pulled a mirror from her bag and checked her mascara. She couldn't share the idea yet. What if someone talked her out of it? Then where would she be? Alexa checked her watch. "Okay. It's time to go in." Leaning heavily on her crutches, Alexa reached for the door leading into Gerrards.

If only she hadn't told on Margo.

"Alexa, you really should have given this Ms. Pik some warning. Maybe she needs another model. . . . "

"She doesn't need another model," Alexa snapped. Quickly, she flashed Mona an apologetic look. There was no point in losing her again. Especially not now. She needed all the support she could get.

Silently, Alexa made her way through the ground floor toward the elevator. She bumped into one woman carrying a huge shopping bag. Alexa muttered an apology and moved on. It wasn't easy. But it wasn't impossible, either. Alexa could feel her determination building. She'd felt this way before. It was like something inside her turning to silvery cold steel.

Alexa held her head high. She smiled to the right. She smiled to the left.

Of course, the big unknown was Ms. Pik.

Could she be convinced her clothes would still look good on Alexa? She looked down at the stylish aqua-and-pink sweatsuit she'd elected to wear.

Then Alexa stared straight ahead.

Ms. Pik would have to believe it.

The steel. She could feel it.

This show was her moment. Nothing was going to take it away.

"Ladies and gentlemen," Margo said, looking into the mirror.

No. That sounded too tentative. Too meek.

"Ladies and gentlemen," she began again. Yes. That was better. "I would like you all to know that today's show, due to the generosity and community spirit of Gerrards, was . . . "

"You want me to listen?" Vivienne asked as she descended on Margo in the Ladies Parlor. "You did it beautifully this morning."

Margo shrugged. Maybe she had. Maybe she hadn't. She just couldn't tell anything anymore.

"You know something, Viv?" She thrust the speech into her friend's hands. "You give it. My heart just isn't in it. I feel disgusting." She glanced at herself in the mirror. "My hair is nowhere, I look fat, and next to everyone else, I look like a donkey."

"No way," Vivienne shook her head. "This is your triumph."

"You mean my tragedy."

Vivienne shrugged. "I heard what happened with your mother last night. She took it pretty badly, huh?"

"I can hardly blame her." Margo felt her shoulders begin to sag. "I kept thinking something would happen to take this whole nightmare away. But it never did. It was Alexa, you know, who told her."

"Yes, I know. But she certainly got punished for that. She's outside with crutches and a sprained ankle, desperately trying to figure out how she can still be in the show." Vivienne started to chuckle. "What a joke."

Margo frowned. "Well, she deserves it. Anyway, I'm sure glad I don't have to face my mother today. That's all I care about."

"Well, not so fast," Vivienne began carefully. "I saw her sitting in the audience. With her friend."

Margo stared at Vivienne blankly. "You must be mistaken."

Vivienne shook her head.

Margo looked up at the ceiling. Why was she there? To humiliate her further? To see Margo ashamed. How could she?

"I'm leaving," Margo announced, suddenly overpowered with the need to run. "I can't give this speech. I can't look at my mother's face. You give it. Say I'm sick. Say I had an emergency. Say whatever you want." Margo moved toward the door, the feeling of panic gripping hard. "I can't do this. . . ."

"Can't do what?" Priscilla sang out as she swung through the door.

"I can't stay here," Margo replied. "I don't know why my mother came. I don't know what she's . . ."

"Planning to see?" Priscilla finished the sentence.

Margo nodded as she tried to push past Priscilla.

"Not so fast." Priscilla shook her head and leaned back against the door so it couldn't be opened.

"Move," Margo insisted frantically. "I'm not kidding. I have to leave."

"Not before you do a little modeling," Priscilla replied simply. She pulled a jean dress out from behind her back.

"What are you talking about?" Margo cried out. "How could you tease me like this?" She eyed the beautifully designed garment with distress. Edged with embroidered ribbon and detailed with tiny pearl buttons, it was heartbreakingly pretty.

"I'm not teasing you," Priscilla said seriously. "You'd better get dressed."

"But I wasn't chosen!" Margo shouted. "Are you nuts?"

"No," Priscilla grinned. "Just a good friend."

Alexa took a deep breath. This was going to take guts. And lots of them. Squeezing Mona's hand, she pushed open the double doors leading into the huge dressing area and looked around. A converted storage area divided up by temporary partitions, it looked like a cosmetic war zone.

Girls were rushing everywhere. Hair half up, half down. Dresses unzipped. One shoe on, one shoe off.

"Alexa, what happened!" Laurie cried out. "You poor thing!" she added as she rushed past to plunge her hand into a basket of rose- and peach-tinted lip gloss.

"Alexa! I had no idea! What are you going to do?" Julie called out from across the room as she studied her black-and-white-striped dress and leggings from behind in a three-way mirror.

Alexa answered no one.

They weren't about to listen, anyway.

She just kept hobbling around the dressing room. Looking.

Planning.

Finally she spotted her.

Her only hope.

Alexa felt the silvery cold steel inside her quiver, ever so slightly.

What a drag — hope's name was Michelle Horne.

"I don't belong up there," Margo sighed as she rushed toward the dressing area.

Priscilla shook her head defiantly. "Wrong. Wrong. Wrong. You do belong up there. But YOU were asked for different reasons. You were asked because you did something important. You contributed valuable work to this event. So did Maria, who helped to pick out the clothes. And so did Joanna, who picked out the music. And that's why you're all modeling 'work' clothes."

Margo shook her head. "It was nice, I guess, of Ms. Pik to think of this."

"What do you mean, Ms. Pik?" Gina asked, catching up from behind. "It wasn't her idea! It was Priscilla's!"

Margo smiled almost shyly at Priscilla. "Thanks. I don't deserve you. I wish I could be more excited about this. I just feel so miserable."

"You had a bad night," Priscilla shrugged. "But you'll see. You'll be coming on somewhere in the middle of the show. It'll be real exciting." She grinned. "You're going to get your moment, Margo. How does that feel?"

"Okay," Margo replied. She forced a big smile. "Good." Actually, it didn't. It felt a little foolish. It felt as if a bunch of people had banded together to try and convince her that what wasn't, was. She wasn't a model type. She wasn't a looker.

This didn't change that for a moment.

"Thanks," she added, smiling warmly at her friends. Still, they'd done a nice thing.

That it didn't work was a secret she would have to keep.

She reached for the dressing room door.

"Alexa, what happened to you?" Michelle whirled around with complete surprise. "Has Ms. Pik seen you?" She unzipped the ice-blue and lavender ski parka she was wearing over matching ski pants. "Boy, this is hot. . . . "

Alexa shook her head, staring intently into Michelle's eyes. "No. She hasn't." Alexa paused. "Michelle, I think we need to clear the air."

Michelle's eyes widened. "Now?"

"Now," Alexa nodded. "You guys hate me. For no reason."

Michelle looked away. "What's this got to do with today? Why are we talking about this now?"

Alexa took a deep breath. It was now or never. "I think you owe me one."

Michelle hesitated, and then shook her head. "I don't know what . . . "

Alexa forced herself to stay calm. There had been a catch in Michelle's voice. She was nervous. She never did like arguing with Alexa.

She smiled at Michelle. "You owe me a chance to prove I'm not the horrible person you all think I am . . . that I'm as nice as the next guy."

Michelle studied her carefully. "You mean like telling Margo's mother she wasn't chosen to model. That kind of nice?"

Alexa flinched. Okay. There it was. Out in the open.

"I don't trust you." Michelle smiled sadly. "I used to. Sort of. But not anymore."

"What about the prom dress I was supposed to wear?" Alexa blurted out. There was no time to waste. Ms. Pik had just walked in. "I could tell you wanted to wear it during rehearsals."

"What about it?" Michelle asked, turning to study herself in the mirror.

Alexa couldn't stand it any longer.

There was no time for a speech.

"I have to model," she cried out softly. "The only way I can do it on crutches is if it fits the outfit. And the only outfit crutches match is a ski outfit. Everyone falls. Everyone breaks legs, twists ankles, sprains knees." She paused. "You have to say yes."

155

Alexa looked to her right and felt her heart leap into her throat. Ms. Pik was on her way over, a stunned look on her face. She whirled around to face Michelle. "It's now or never, make up your mind."

Michelle continued staring into the mirror for a long moment. Finally, she turned to face Alexa. "Isn't that prom dress you're wearing royal blue?"

Alexa nodded eagerly. "Your best color."

Michelle grinned.

Alexa smiled. She'd done it. She'd pulled it off.

Michelle turned to look around the room. She tilted her head slightly and began to suck on her lower lip. Finally, she turned back to Alexa.

"I have to think," she said. "Wait here."

A moment later, she brushed past Ms. Pik, Mona, and Laurie, and tore across the large room.

Alexa stood helplessly in one spot, watching Ms. Pik draw ever closer.

20

Margo took one step into the dressing room, and wanted to leave.

Everything look so dramatic. So confused. So glamorous.

So unlike her.

Shoes were everywhere. Mascara tubes littered the floor. Little squares of blue and green eye shadow were strewn on the tables. Hysterical girls spun around the room, pulling on stockings, squeezing into bras, wrestling with buttons.

Margo looked down at the jean dress draped across her arm. She looked at Priscilla, who was standing close by her side. She closed her eyes and imagined her mother sitting in the audience.

She shook her head. It was a no go.

"I can't," she said simply. She pushed the dress toward Priscilla. "It probably won't fit, anyway. Look at the waist."

"You can," Priscilla replied, grabbing her arm. "And it will." She pulled Margo over to the side in an unoccupied spot behind a giant plant.

"Here. Let's get you dressed fast, and then we'll steal a spot at one of the mirrors and Gina will fix your makeup." Without waiting for an answer, she and Gina began pulling off Margo's sweater.

"This is ridiculous. This isn't me. . . . " Margo protested, much to her surprise not entirely meaning it. It was kind of nice having matters taken out of her own hands.

"Who is it, then?" Vivienne laughed, suddenly appearing by her side. "Margaret Thatcher?" She laughed again. "Stop complaining for once, will you? You're getting what you want! Your problem is that you're so ungrateful!"

Margo looked away. No one understood. It was nice everyone wanted her to be happy, but no one understood this was happening the wrong way. This was a booby prize. Couldn't they see that?

She was miserable.

She was nervous.

She was out of place.

She began fastening the tiny little pearl buttons. The dress fit perfectly.

Margo peeked around the plant to look for a mirror.

One was half-empty a few feet away. Margo walked over.

She looked.

She was scared.

She was confused.

But suddenly she was something else, too.
She was excited.

Alexa stood perfectly still watching Ms. Pik advance toward her. She felt like a soldier, at war, with no weapon.

It wasn't fair.

But that was okay. She'd toughed out worse things.

She smiled softly. A nervous-looking Mona was now rushing protectively to her side, only a few steps behind Ms. Pik.

"Alexa!" Ms. Pik cried out. "How terrible for you! When did this happen?" She was standing next to Alexa now, her hand resting sympathetically on Alexa's shoulder.

"Yesterday," Alexa began carefully, "but don't worry, because I can still . . . "

"You must be in so much pain," Ms. Pik sighed. "And when I think of how pretty you looked in that prom dress. . . . "

"Well, that's okay," Alexa broke in. "But don't worry about that dress, because someone else can wear it and then I . . . "

"Oh, sweetheart, I know someone else can wear it," Ms. Pik nodded. "How sweet that you were worried about that!"

"Well, actually," Alexa continued, "I wasn't finished." For a moment, she almost started laughing. Ms. Pik didn't have a clue with whom she was dealing.

"Someone else can wear the dress, and I can wear what they're wearing."

"Excuse me?" Ms. Pik answered, obviously confused. "Whatever do you mean?"

"I mean," Alexa answered, suddenly aware her voice had started to quiver. She paused for a moment and took a deep breath. "I think that Michelle Horne is going to switch with me. I could wear the ski outfit and still model with crutches. Skiers are always on crutches." She paused and nudged Mona. "Wouldn't that just be perfect?"

For an agonizing moment, Mona simply stared at her.

Alexa felt a sharp jab of panic. She forced herself to smile fetchingly at Ms. Pik. "Mona just can't believe what a great idea this is!"

She tapped Mona's shoe with her crutch.

Nothing. Alexa felt her resolve slipping away. Just at that moment, Mona seemed to wake up.

"Yes . . . yes . . . " Mona suddenly sputtered, her face lighting up into a huge grin. "It's a great idea, Ms. Pik."

Alexa nodded enthusiastically. She was getting a stomachache.

"I don't know." Ms. Pik paused. "I really don't. Has Michelle agreed to this?"

"It'll work," Alexa assured her, ignoring the

160

question. "It could be great!" She looked around the room. "Oh, there's a mirror with no one in front of it. Better hurry over and fix my makeup." And with that, she whirled around and started hobbling away.

Ms. Pik did not look happy. Alexa squared her shoulders. Too bad.

I am like a steamroller, she said to herself. Determined. Powerful. Ready to flatten anything in my way.

She took a seat. This day could have only one outcome. Her parents were out there. Barry was out there. The world was out there. She'd convinced them all that she'd be in the show. Somehow.

Ms. Pik would simply have to cope.

And Michelle would simply have to give in.

And that, was that.

"There!" Gina announced, waving the eyeliner brush through the air with a flourish. "You look fantastic."

Margo leaned in closer to the mirror. Maybe.

"You look like a model," Priscilla said, nodding her head somberly.

"Isn't that just the best thing?" Vivienne sang out in a high-pitched voice dripping with sarcasm. "Aren't you lucky?"

Margo started giggling. "Okay. Okay. I get it,

Vivienne." She stood up and moved over to a full-length mirror that had just been vacated. "What do you think my mother will think?"

"What do you think?" Priscilla said, motioning for everyone else to be quiet.

Margo hesitated. "I'm not sure." She paused. "Pretty good, actually." She frowned. It was a terrible thing not to know what to think of oneself.

"Girls, quick," Michelle whispered urgently as she descended upon them from the other side of the room. "You guys saw Alexa? She sprained her ankle. She can't model the prom dress."

"What a tragedy," Vivienne smiled. "I can't take it."

"Well, wait," Michelle shook her head. "That's not the point. The point is, she wants me to model her prom dress and she would model my ski outfit because, after all, skiers walk around with crutches a lot. . . . " She looked from face to face. "If I don't say yes, she probably will miss the show. What do you think I should do?"

Gina shrugged. "Do you like the dress?"

Michelle nodded. "I do. More than this." She looked down at her outfit with a frown.

"But do we want to do Alexa a favor?" Vivienne yelped. "Especially after what she just did to Margo?"

Margo looked up with surprise. For a second, she actually had to think of what it was Alexa had done.

"What do you think?" Gina asked, turning to Margo.

"I'm not sure," Margo sighed. She studied her reflection thoughtfully. She glanced at Michelle, who was looking at her with an odd expression on her face.

"You really love that prom dress?" Margo asked softly.

Michelle hesitated. "I can do without it," she responded unconvincingly.

Margo nodded and looked back at her own reflection.

The truth was, despite what Alexa had intended, not everything had turned out quite so badly. In fact, in a very small, secret way she was almost grateful to her.

Unless it turned out she was about to make a fool of herself. Margo took the hairbrush out of Gina's hand and nervously ran it through the one frizzy spot on her head, in the back, to the right.

Well, her moment had finally come. The daughter of Miss Georgia Peach strutting her stuff. Sure, it hadn't come about the classic Kelly way. But then there was nothing all that classic about Margo.

She turned to study Michelle, who was now watching her expectantly. Almost, Margo thought, hopefully. Her mind wandered once more.

Alexa was the daughter Aurora should have had.

Margo hated Alexa for it. She envied her terribly.

Alexa deserved nothing from her. Absolutely nothing.

But Michelle was her trusted friend.

Margo looked into Michelle's eyes and smiled.

On balance, loyalty was worth more than revenge.

21

Alexa stood, frozen, in the middle of the dressing room. She felt as if she couldn't move.

"Loosen up," Mona urged her. "This isn't like you."

"I'm not me," Alexa snapped. "I can't do this."

"Sure you can," Mona responded, more softly this time. "You're Alexa Craft. Nothing gets you down. Besides, you look beautiful."

"Did you see Michelle? Did you see how beautiful and graceful she looked?" Alexa whispered. "That should have been me! I hate her!"

"Alexa Craft," Mona practically choked. "Are you kidding me? How could you!"

Alexa looked down at the ice-blue and lavender ski outfit she was now wearing. It was hard to know if anyone would even notice how great she looked. What with the crutches and all.

"This was probably a big mistake," Alexa sighed, feeling herself begin to crumble. "I probably just should have accepted this wasn't meant to be. Look at everybody!" She picked up one crutch and made a semicircle with it in the air. "They all look so . . . so . . . perfect. Barry is going to think I look ridiculous, and my parents just wasted their time."

"No, they didn't," Mona assured her. "Now look, you're next. You have to remember something. I know this is hard for you, but work on it." She paused. "Half of being pretty is feeling pretty. Half of looking good is feeling good. You never think about that because you happen to have been born beautiful. But it's true. Now, you look great. If you go out there and do what you intended — look the part of the pretty skier who had an accident — then that's what you'll look like." Mona giggled. "And remember, guys love to help pretty girls in trouble!"

Alexa looked at Mona affectionately. "I don't know what I'd do without you, Mona." She looked away. "In fact, I've missed you a lot. You've been so busy. . . . "

Mona nodded sadly. "I missed you, too. You perk me up. You make me laugh." Then she shot Alexa a stern expression. "I also still wish you'd help me with this debate."

Alexa shook her head in bewilderment. "I don't know what you're talking about. What could I do?"

Mona grinned. "What you're about to do, which you do better than anyone. You can show me how to make people think you feel good. You have this great way of looking and seeming confident. If I don't learn how you do it, I'm going to lose this debate. Everyone tells me I act like a mouse!"

Alexa smiled sadly. "I sure can put on a show, huh?"

Mona slipped an arm around her and squeezed. "Yes, you can. But goodness, Alexa. Some of it has to be real. You've got so much going for you!"

"And now," the voice echoed from the main room back toward the curtained area, "we have Ms. Alexa Craft modeling a spirited outfit just right for the pristine white ski slopes of Vermont . . . whether you're speeding down the mountain, or nursing a few injuries. . . . "

There was a brief titter from the audience, and Alexa felt herself being gently pushed forward by her friend.

She took a deep breath and, for an instant, closed her eyes.

Whatever had possessed her to do this?

Margo peeked out from behind the curtain and spotted her mother sitting with Lily Bardavid. She looked tense. Margo shook her head. Mrs. Warner had no idea Margo was going to model. Why was she here?

"Feeling okay?" Gina whispered as the two of them watched Betsy Kulkin practically dance down the runway in a short blue skirt and matching sweater with glitter everywhere. "Don't you just love this music!"

Margo shrugged. Actually, she was too nervous to love anything. Anxiously, she looked down at her shoes. They were borrowed from the store and didn't exactly fit right. They looked good with the dress, though. She turned around and took a few steps to the left. They felt as if they might fall off.

"I think I'm going to trip in these. . . . "

"No. You won't. Just kind of hang onto them with your toes," Gina replied. "They're probably only a half size too big."

"Mine felt too big, too," Michelle commented.

Margo nodded and grinned at her friend. "Well, you looked perfect out there." She reached out to squeeze Michelle's hand. Then she straightened the shoulders of her dress and ran her tongue over her lips. "Do I have enough lip gloss on? My lips feel dry."

"You do," Vivienne whispered. "In fact, you look as if you left your lips at a grease factory overnight."

"What!" Margo cried out softly. "What do you mean?"

"Don't listen to her!" Priscilla said, laughing out loud. "She's just trying to get you to loosen up!"

Margo nodded and looked away. It was almost her turn.

Okay, a voice inside her head whispered softly. Close your eyes. Relax. Make believe those people out there are all your friends. Pretend you are an experienced model. You've just flown in from Paris. This is just a small thing you've agreed to do for a friend. How nice of you.

Margo opened her eyes and smiled. Yes. This was nothing out of the ordinary. Just a day's work. Nothing more. She ran a hand through her thick, lustrous hair. She peered down at her shapely slim legs. She ran a hand over her flat stomach and trim hips.

"And now please welcome the girl who gave real meaning to this event. She is the one who brought together the Port Andrews Committee for the Homeless and Gerrards, Ms. Margo Warner. You will be hearing from her later. But for now, here she is modeling a delicately detailed demin dress that can travel from a busy work or school day to a casual dance."

Margo smiled shakily at her friends, and then stepped forward. The voice came back. Remember, a Paris model. You do this twice a day.

Then the voice faded.

And Margo Warner, terrified but determined, stepped forward, and began, for better or for worse, to model.

For a brief moment, Alexa stood, poised, at the top of the runway, smiled, and looked around the room. It didn't help.

She didn't feel pretty.

She could see her parents. Actually, just her

father. He was smiling brightly at her. Alexa looked away quickly. Funny. She actually felt a little shy.

And then she started forward. After all, she had to.

"Alexa is wearing an ice-blue and lavender, nylon and spandex ski outfit with snug wrists and a zip-on hood. A flattering hip-length jacket . . . "

Alexa tossed back her blonde hair and tried to keep her smile sincere. What was it Mona had said? Yes. She would look pretty and happy if she acted that way. . . .

Even if people did laugh. Even if they did wonder why she was there.

Her eyes scanned the room for Barry. She couldn't find him. That was just as well. Seeing him would have made her even more nervous. Not knowing where he sat was better.

Like a robot, she took one step after another, the soft thud of the crutches accompanying her every move. Alexa glanced to the right. She'd heard someone laughing softly.

She fought back tears. This was not the moment she'd dreamt of. Why hadn't she let it go? Darn Mimi and her crazy ideas . . .

"What a lovely sense of humor she must have," a voice whispered to her left.

Alexa whirled around with surprise to spot a group of women she'd never seen before.

Alexa continued forward.

Suddenly, to her right, she heard someone softly clap. "Good for you," a voice called out gently. "Not just pretty, but determined, too."

"A real trouper," she heard from somewhere behind. "And the outfit looks great."

Alexa kept her eyes forward, completely unsure of what to feel.

The question was, did she still look beautiful? Would her parents and Barry finally see . . .

"Notice the contrasting pattern lining of the jacket. An unusual feature to be sure . . . "

Alexa hesitated for a moment, and then came to a full stop. She transferred a crutch to one side and, with her free hand, unzipped and opened her jacket.

Someone began to clap.

"Thatta way!" a familiar voice called out. Alexa glanced around the room quickly, but couldn't figure out where it had come from.

Reaching now the end of the runway, she turned around smoothly.

"Probably, a real go-getter," a voice whispered.

Alexa hesitated. Okay, but did she look . . .

Suddenly, the thought simply stopped. It was as if someone clicked off the radio. The tape broke. As if the recording had simply worn out.

Alexa held back her shoulders and lifted her chin.

Actually, it was unbelievable.

A red-letter day.

For the first time in her life, she was being admired for something else besides her looks.

She did have guts. She did have a sense of humor. She did "go get" things.

Alexa could feel her spirits soaring.

There were so many things inside her . . .

And then, suddenly, she saw him.

The person whose familiar voice had rung out just moments ago.

He blew her a big kiss.

Alexa tossed back her hair, feeling more beautiful than she ever had before.

In fact, she had to fight the urge to leave the runway and fly into his arms.

Suddenly, he looked SO cute.

Yes. He was going to make a wonderful boyfriend.

Alexa grinned.

David was a go-getter, too.

Listening to the rhythm of a Whitney Houston song, Margo began walking briskly down the runway.

It felt bizarre. She trained her eyes on the clock directly in front of her on the far wall and willed herself to keep moving.

You can do this, the soft voice encouraged her. You look fine. Don't forget, you did make callbacks.

"Notice the silk embroidered ribbon edging on the collar and cuffs. . . . "

Margo smiled. She felt as if her arms were made of lead balloons. She placed them in her pockets. Models did that a lot.

"Isn't she pretty!" a voice whispered from somewhere to her right. "Just adorable."

Margo was stunned.

She had to fight the urge to turn around and see if another girl had stepped out onto the runway.

A moment later, she realized that was impossible.

One hand came out of her pocket and began to swing at her side. It felt lighter now.

"Isn't that a lovely dress. Just right for her slim figure," another woman murmured, sitting very close to the runway.

Margo couldn't quite believe it. She almost started laughing.

She was nearing the end of the runway. Out of the corner of her eye Margo could see her mother.

She looked completely blank. As if she had no emotion at all.

Margo quickly turned away.

Of course. This was not enough. Just as she thought.

She was at the midway point now. Margo turned and started back up the runway.

"Dynamite looking," a voice from the audience called out.

Margo smiled.

It was incredible. She was modeling. She looked like she belonged. And it was so easy!

Margo looked from right to left and smiled broadly.

What a kick. Everyone was staring at her. Everyone was admiring her!

She ran a hand quickly through her thick dark curls.

It felt so . . . weird!

Margo took a deep breath and measured the distance to the curtain. She still had a way to go.

Oh, well. What a . . .

For a moment, Margo could not find the right words. Nothing seemed to fit. "Spectacular moment" didn't do it. "Incredible time" wasn't right, either.

Margo was almost finished now, as she felt herself moving smoothly and confidently along the runway.

And then the phrase came to her.

"Unforgettable experience."

Margo burst through the curtains into the arms of The Practically Popular Crowd.

"Well! How was it?" Priscilla exclaimed.

"Your moment! You magnificent thing, you!" Vivienne laughed.

"You looked great," Gina informed her. "Like a professional!"

Margo smiled.

How could she tell them?

It had felt great. She'd felt very pretty. She'd felt very admired.

But she'd felt something else, too.

She'd felt just a little ridiculous.

A little out of place.

Like a sea gull in a cornfield.

But not because she wasn't pretty enough.

No. Not at all.

The truth was, she couldn't wait to give her speech.

She couldn't wait to feel like the real Margo Warner.

22

"And so, thank you very much in advance for any purchase you may make that adds to the Port Andrews Committee for the Homeless funds."

Margo stepped back from the microphone and, with a little bow, walked behind the curtains.

There was no one there except a few girls she hardly knew getting back into their own clothes. Everyone else had stepped to the front to hear her and Ms. Pik speak.

Feeling empty, Margo walked over to a makeup table and began applying a touch of cold cream to her face. She looked down at the cluttered tray of makeup and smiled softly. It certainly was a glamorous business, this modeling. She looked up at her reflection, suddenly stopping the circular motion she was using to remove her makeup.

Mrs. Warner had arrived.

Margo watched her approach in the mirror, trying hard to stay calm.

"You gave a lovely speech," Mrs. Warner said softly, pulling a chair up next to her daughter.

"Thank you," Margo barely whispered.

"You also looked beautiful up there."

Margo smiled. "I'm glad."

"You see. You can do it. . . . " Mrs. Warner continued.

Margo tensed. "It was a special thing."

"I know," Mrs. Warner said, putting both hands in the air as if to stop her daughter. "I figured that. Still, you looked great up there."

Margo shrugged.

Mrs. Warner was silent for a moment. She twisted a handkerchief in her lap.

"Margo, I've been pushy. I'm sorry. I have wanted you to carry on some silly tradition and . . . "

"It's not silly, Mom." Margo interrupted. "I wanted it, too, in a way. It's just not me."

"I know that," Mrs. Warner sighed.

Margo looked away. There it was again. She'd let her down.

"You're something else altogether. And I haven't been smart enough to give you what you deserve."

Margo turned around with surprise.

"Like what?"

Mrs. Warner smiled and touched her daughter's cheek. "Like my respect for being a caring, intelligent girl with a wonderful personality and her own beautiful brand of Kelly girl looks. That's what."

Margo felt the tears beginning to form.

"You mean that? Really?"

Mrs. Warner nodded. "I do." She paused. "I suppose I've been hiding from my own problems, too. I never did think I had much to offer other than my looks. They came to mean everything to me. I mean, that's what won your father over," she added with a soft smile. "But you don't need that. You are SO capable."

"But Mom, you're a very good person! And such a good real estate agent!" Margo interrupted, almost surprised by how much she meant it.

"I suppose," Mrs. Warner sighed. "But my heart really isn't in it." She paused. "Not like you and your politics. Of course, I still don't think you allow yourself to be quite the beauty you are. And I don't know why you resist going to some of those parties I hear you girls talking about. . . . "

Margo smiled forlornly at her mother.

Something this big couldn't just turn around overnight.

"You are a Kelly, you know, Margo, no matter what cause you're championing!" her mother went on, with a broad proud smile.

Margo did not smile back. Instead, she took a deep breath and blurted something out that she'd hardly been able to say to herself even during the quietest, most private moments.

"You know, Mom, I'm a Warner girl, too," she murmured as tears suddenly sprang to her eyes. Quickly, she looked away from her mother, afraid of the memories the shared pain might conjure up.

There was a deafening silence. Finally, she turned back and was completely surprised to see a bright and beautiful smile upon her mother's face.

"What a lovely thought," Mrs. Warner said softly, "for both of us." And then her eyes, too, welled up with tears.

Alexa stood outside Gerrards feeling positively wonderful. Powerful. Interesting. Exciting. Important.

And then pretty. In that order.

She looked affectionately at David.

He gazed back at her.

Here was someone who liked her for her.

She looked around at the crowd. So many mothers. Minus one.

"If you'd told her what your plans were, she might have gotten away," Mona whispered, reading her friend's thoughts. "Your father said she had a crisis at work. Who could blame her for thinking you weren't going to make it up there?"

"There's the car," Alexa replied matter-of-factly, ignoring Mona's words. Excuses, excuses. Her mother should have known. "Let's go celebrate. An early dinner!"

Alexa looked around. She was surrounded by people who were so proud of her. So impressed with her. So pleased with her . . . Why let anything ruin it? She frowned. Alissa Craft had made a mistake. Not her.

Alexa squeezed David's hand as they stood close together.

She looked at his lips and tried to imagine what it would be like to kiss him.

She tried to imagine what he would say when he got her alone.

She tried to figure out where Barry was.

Not that it mattered so much. It was just that getting stood up was . . . well . . . no small thing.

It certainly wasn't something she wanted to get around.

It would kill her reputation.

Just blow it to smithereens.

"So where's creepo Barry?" Alexa asked as casually as she could manage.

"Didn't think you were going to actually do it, so he didn't come." David shrugged. "He doesn't know what you're made of."

Alexa nodded. That was for sure.

"Well, you certainly get what you want, don't

you, Alexa?" a voice announced from a few feet away.

Alexa whirled around to find Vivienne standing there with a smug smile on her face.

Alexa forced herself to be reasonable. "It was nice of Michelle to offer me her outfit," she said simply.

Vivienne nodded. "It was her decision." She paused. "By the way. Have you apologized to Margo for your behavior during this event?" She smiled at David.

Alexa looked away. Why couldn't Vivienne keep her big mouth shut? What happened was between her and Margo. David didn't have to hear this.

Alexa turned toward David, only to find him eyeing her curiously.

"What behavior?" he asked, a knowing smile threatening to break out.

Alexa quickly flashed him her most meaningful look. "Just girl stuff. Forget it."

Vivienne grinned. "Girl stuff. What an interesting way to describe it, Alexa. . . . "

Alexa nodded. "I guess I'm just an interesting kind of girl," she said coolly, and then turned her back.

But not before she saw Vivienne give David the once over.

She couldn't control herself.

"See something you're interested in?" she said, looking over her shoulder with a sly smile.

Vivienne nodded solemnly. "I guess that's why Barry and Gina are playing tennis tomorrow." She cocked her head to one side, grinned from ear to ear, and then turned and walked away.

"Ignore her," David smiled at Alexa warmly.

"Of course," Alexa smiled back, as if nothing else mattered but him.

Which simply wasn't true.

Barry and Gina mattered tremendously.

They were simply unacceptable.

Barry and an almost popular something girl? Instead of her?

It was a matter of principle.

It really had to be stopped.

And that was the thing which, unfortunately, mattered most of all to Alexa Craft as she stood clasping hands with a guy she liked more than anyone else she'd ever met.

Look for the next
Practically Popular Crowd book:
Keeping Secrets

"By the way, what was that with Lucas yesterday?" Priscilla asked. "I couldn't believe it! I meant to call you last night."

Gina hesitated and then very slowly shook her head. "That was something, wasn't it," she murmured with disinterest. Boredom.

It was amazing. She was lying, and it was coming so easily. She was being so . . . secretive.

It was actually horribly exciting.

"What did he want?" Priscilla persisted. "I saw you guys talking."

"He just was asking me about my running times. That's all."

So many lies. Gina looked from girl to girl, smiling evenly. And why not? No one was getting hurt.

About the Author

MEG F. SCHNEIDER was practically popular when she was growing up in New York City. She remembers feeling very excited and scared, insecure and confident, hurt and happy . . . sometimes all at once! And that is why she created **The Practically Popular Crowd**. She hopes it will help readers understand themselves better.

Ms. Schneider is also the author of the Apple Paperback *The Ghost in the Picture*.

She graduated from Tufts University and received a master's degree in counseling psychology from Columbia University. She lives in Westchester County, New York, with her husband and two young sons.